The Badge and the Bible

Terry Burns

LONE MESA PUBLISHING

The Badge and the Bible
ISBN 978-0692548158
Copyright © 2015 Terry Burns
All rights reserved.

DEDICATION

Sheriff Buck Green, the main character in this book is fictional, but he embodies many of the characteristics of several fine law enforcement people I have been fortunate to know and who gave me some insight in this book, primarily Sheriff Buck Jackson of Reeves County, Texas. But primarily it's dedicated to my son, Bryan Burns, retired detective lieutenant of the Carlsbad, New Mexico, Police Department. Not only a good cop, but the best son a man could have.

I dedicate this book to them.

PROLOGUE

Buck Green is a small town Sheriff who pastors a church on the side ... or is he a small church pastor that also wears a badge? It is a question Buck struggles to answer. Walking the line between the badge and the Bible can be difficult and involves many choices and much soul-searching. Not all of the questions have been answered.

Chapter 1

Sheriff Buck Green intended to have a leisurely lunch when the radio blared the words "Officer needs assistance... shots fired!" The thin electronic voice belonged to Clear Creek's only female officer, Carol Tatum. No message got a lawman's adrenaline pumping like that dreaded call.

The radio added, "Officer needs assistance! I'm pinned down behind my unit at third and Jefferson!"

Buck heard sirens blaring in the distance as he backed out of the drive-in, tires squealing, one-handing the rest of his hamburger. The half-consumed cup of hot coffee still sat between his legs.

He tossed the burger, keeping the wrapper, then did the same with the remaining coffee, grimacing as it distributed itself evenly down the side of the patrol car. *Birds gotta eat too,* he thought.

The disposal project held Buck's attention a shade too long, and he found himself running up on a red Toyota. He flipped on the top beacons to whip around the little car without reducing speed. *No point in being Sheriff if I can't have a little fun now and then,* he thought. Buck liked to drive with the light-bar on, but seldom got the chance.

Clearing the car, he stepped down even harder, and the powerful engine roared like a pride of angry lions. People in small towns still yielded right-of-way to an emergency vehicle, so he had a clear run ... and he used it.

As he slid to a stop beside Carol's unit, a bullet smashed into his windshield. He pulled the shotgun out of the rack and jumped out to duck down beside Carol. Buck dressed more like a working rancher than a cop, favoring blue jeans and checked, western-cut shirts instead of the khaki uniform shirt his deputies wore. If it weren't for the big gold badge pinned to a leather flap in his pocket, people might have trouble figuring him to be the law. Buck didn't fit into a pigeonhole because he was more than a small-town Sheriff. He also pastored a small church on the outskirts of Clear Creek.

He liked to say he served both the badge and the Bible.

Buck worked the slide on the shotgun. It seemed inappropriate to him for even a part-time preacher to wear a handgun, but he had no problem being a first-class hunter with the weapon he held in his hands.

You all right?" he said.

Her face contorted as she nodded. "I got hit. Thank God my vest saved me." She showed him the indentation in front of her arm. "Man, it felt like getting kicked by a mule. I think I've got a couple of cracked ribs. I don't know what would have happened if Mike hadn't driven up in the back and diverted their attention."

"He's in the back?" Buck looked in that direction even though it was impossible for him to see anything.

"Yeah, I talked to him a minute ago. He came in as backup on the original domestic disturbance call. That's what brought me, a DD call a couple of doors down."

She leaned back against the front wheel of the unit as she made a futile gesture with her hands. "At first I didn't know what had happened, stunned, I guess. I suppose these people thought I was coming after them and opened up on me."

"Why?" He studied her face. She had lost her hat, and her dishwater blonde hair crowded her face, but she was calm and disciplined, an ex-marine to the core. He hadn't been under fire before... but she had.

"I think we stumbled into some kind of drug deal or something. Whatever's going on, they're pretty paranoid about it."

"I reckon so, firing on sight." Buck grimaced, at his age he couldn't squat very long, and his legs already complained.

If she saw his discomfort, she gave no sign of it. "At any rate, we've got them boxed. They aren't going anywhere."

Buck nodded. "What makes you think this is a drug thing? We haven't had any signs of that in town, outside of catching those punkers with marijuana joints, that is. Country folks generally don't take to that stuff."

"Yeah, trying to catch somebody underage with beer is more of a problem." Carol shrugged. "I don't really know why I thought that, it's just what popped into my head."

Buck eased to a sitting position and leaned back against the unit. His legs continued to torment him, "I suppose that could be the case. I'm positive the Interstate is a drug pipeline running right past us, whether we've seen signs of it or not. I figured we were just too small to get caught up in it."

The distracted look on his face passed and changed to a look of concern. "At any rate, you've done a good job. I don't guess you'd let me send you over to the hospital to get checked out, would you?"

The look she returned would freeze water. His grin spread to his eyes. "I didn't think so."

The radio crackled, and Mike's voice came on with, "Carol, Kenneth and two DPS troopers are back here with me now."

Buck reached over to get the microphone out of the patrol car, grateful for the chance to uncoil. "Okay, you sit tight now."

"Sure thing, Sheriff, didn't know you were there."

"I'm here. Dispatch, you copying this?" Buck released the button and got a positive response, then spoke to the dispatcher. "Penny, if you would, look up the phone number for this place. Call the phone company if you have to. I'm in the mood to talk to somebody."

He dialed the number she gave him into his mobile phone. Someone answered. "Morning," Buck said, "You folks is a mite testy in there, ain't you?"

"Who is this?" The husky voice had an unfamiliar accent, from back east, maybe.

"This is Sheriff Green. We're getting tired of sitting out here providing you boys with target practice. Why don't you pitch your hardware out the door and come out with your hands up, before you go and make me mad?"

"Not in this lifetime." The accent continued to puzzle him. "Here's how things are going to go down, Sheriff. We're going to bust out of here and see how you backwoods yokels stack up against some real firepower. If you don't want to get some people hurt, you better back off and give us a road out."

"Your choice, but I gotta tell you, my folks can hit birds on the wing with these shotguns, and I guarantee you'll never get halfway to your car no matter how much lead you throw out."

Buck paused for effect. "Now, let me explain to you how I think this deal is going to 'go down,' as you put it. First, we're not going to put any shot into the air without a definite target, but if we see one, we'll hit it. Second, I'm not going to risk any officers by trying to rush you."

"Sounds like a standoff to me, Sheriff," the voice said.

"No, that's not exactly it, either. I don't plan to sit out here for a month while you decide whether or not to give up. I called over for Joe Bob to come running with that old bulldozer he's got. It's dang near the size of that whole house. When it gets here, I'm going to get up on top and drive that hoss right through the middle of the place."

He paused again, then added, "Oh yeah, you folks feel free to waste as many bullets as you want on the big blade on the front. When I get through, the guys I have out back are real fine shots, particularly those state troopers, and they can pick off anything left over. If anything *is* left over, which I doubt will be the case."

Buck glanced over at Carol. The deputy had a quizzical look on her face as if she didn't know if Buck was serious or not.

The phone was still silent, so Buck added, "I guess that's about it. I've always wanted to take a house down with one of those things. I guess to be fair, though, I ought to give you a few minutes to come out. I figure it'll take about five more minutes for the bulldozer to get over here, time starting about... now. It's your choice, so you let me know what you think." Carol's quizzical look faded, and she shook her head in disbelief.

There was still no response. After a minute or two, Buck told Carol, "I guess it ain't too smart for us to be sitting here with our back to them like we were on coffee break. They could slip right over here and do all sort of nasty things to us."

Carol started to get up and look, but he restrained her with a hand on her arm. "Wait." He took his hat off and balanced it on the barrel of the shotgun. "This always works for Roy Rogers," he said as he hoisted it slightly over the fender. A shot sounded and a small hole appeared in the hat, spinning it around on the barrel.

He pulled it down and scowled at it. "Rats! They never hit Roy's good hat."

Carol sighed. "Looks like they're calling your bluff."

"What bluff?" Buck gestured with a nod of his head. She looked down the street to see a big D-4 Caterpillar bulldozer rumbling toward them with Joe Bob Taylor at the controls.

Chapter 2

The big cat's engine grumbled as it idled. Buck kept the patrol car between him and the house, and he crouched low as he ran over to it. He slipped up onto the seat beside the grinning driver, safe behind the big blade.

"I can't believe you want to do this," Joe Bob said. "Why'd you decide on a bulldozer?"

"I'd rather have a Sherman tank if you've got one."

Joe Bob patted his pockets. "Not on me." Joe Bob had the same boyish good looks and perennial smile that had served him well back in his high school quarterback days. He may have been middle-aged, but he was one of, if not *the* most eligible bachelor in town.

"This'll have to do then." Buck studied the controls. His bushy eyebrows contorted into an almost-solid line. "I run one of these critters in the army, but you might check me out on it anyway."

"Why don't you let me do this?" Joe Bob's eyes flashed with anticipation and excitement. "I really would enjoy it."

"Would you enjoy being sued if this turns out to be a bum idea?"

"Good point! Right, your show."

Buck listened to a quick explanation of the controls. "Okay, okay, it's all coming back to me," He worked the levers and the foot pedals, made the big machine move slightly as he got the feel of it. "I don't have to be in any kind of hurry anyway. It's not like I have to get a run at the house or anything."

Joe Bob jumped off the big tread to the ground. "You're only bluffing anyway, right?"

Buck grinned. "That's strictly up to them."

◊

Joe Bob ducked behind the unit with Carol. "You believing this?"

She shrugged. "The Sheriff is nothing if not colorful."

Today had started out so normal. Joe Bob couldn't believe he was now crouching behind a car with people on the other side of it shooting it him. He should have just been down at the five and dime having coffee at the lunch counter by now.

He looked at her intently, "Are you all right?"

"Yes, not the first time I've been shot. I was wounded in action twice. Once my flak jacket took it, like now. Later I wasn't so lucky and took a little shrapnel."

Jim Bob grimaced as he studied her face. She said it so matter-of-factly. He thought he needed to revise his opinion of this little lady. She wasn't the petite little thing she appeared to be. This girl had some iron in her backbone. "I feel kind of naked out here."

"You can fondle the Sheriff's shotgun if it'll make you feel better."

She handed it to him. He worked the slide just enough to see that there was a shell in the chamber. "Thanks, at least I feel like I can protect myself now."

"You don't trust me to protect you?"

"I'm starting to."

◊

Buck grinned as he worked the levers. The stack belched black smoke as the cat inched forward, the vibration jarring every bone in his body. He brought the blade up for cover as he pointed it toward the house. Several shots bounced harmlessly off the heavy metal.

Buck took the cat up the curb and into the yard. He eased back on the throttle, punched the redial on his cellular phone and listened to the ringing tone. "You people keep shooting at me, you really are gonna make me mad," he said when someone answered.

"You don't scare me," the man's voice said. "I know you're bluffing."

"I was so hoping you'd say that."

Buck put the phone down to hit the throttle and inch forward. The rails on the porch gave way, then the porch roof collapsed.

He stopped to touch the redial button again. "Last chance."

"You're bluffing." This time the voice didn't sound so confident.

"Your call, you got ten seconds... TEN... NINE... Buck began to goose the throttle at regular intervals, VAROOM, VAROOM... he could hear things falling off the walls inside... EIGHT... SEVEN...

Buck raised the blade and dropped it. It smashed the concrete of the porch as if it were nothing. He quickly put the blade back up in the protective position. SIX... FIVE... FOUR...

He said, "I'm hanging up now, good luck to you people, you're surely going to need it."

Buck jacked the throttle up, grabbed hold of the levers and moved forward... He grinned. Suddenly a chair came through the front window, and someone waved a white cloth out the broken window.

Buck dialed them again. "You trying to get in touch with me?"

"You're crazy, man, you're completely crazy."

"You just now figuring that out?"

"You'll do it, won't you? You'll really do it?"

"One way to find out."

"I don't want to find out. Have your people hold their fire. We're coming out."

Buck sighed. He realized he was actually disappointed, but, after all, he was a preacher. He ought not to think such things. "Guns first," he said, "then hands on top of your head."

They came out, single file, hands on their heads. Buck called behind him, "Keep 'em covered, Joe Bob. Officer Tatum, I believe this collar belongs to you."

Joe Bob stood and worked the slide for emphasis, the ejected shell bounced down the sidewalk as he swung the barrel toward the trio that lifted their hands high as they came out of the house.

Carol smiled like a possum caught under a porch light, pulled herself up to her full five foot one, and said, "Keep those fingers laced together and get down on your knees." They complied.

The officers covering the back came running. One asked, "What do you need, Sheriff?"

"Officer Tatum is the arresting officer, fellows." He worked to restrain a grin. "You boys see if she needs any help."

◊

Buck stopped by the church on his way back to the office, just to check on things. He loved this old converted one-room schoolhouse on the outskirts of town. He'd originally signed on as deputy sheriff to make ends meet when his small congregation couldn't pay enough to maintain a full-time pastor. Over the years, the job at the department grew until he found himself elected Sheriff. Now, his law enforcement job took so much time that his ministerial duties had become the part-time function.

Every now and then, he entertained thoughts about moving to a bigger church, one that could pay a living wage so he could minister full time. But the thoughts didn't last long. He really didn't *fit* in a big-church environment. The people in his little church were *his* kind of people. That meant he was just where he belonged.

He wandered to the pulpit, checked that the floors had been swept. And thought about the sermon he had to write for Sunday. Could he use anything from today's encounter as a lesson there?

One thing was constant here, no matter which collar he wore: he knew these people, each and every one. They went to work when they were supposed to. On Sundays, they were in their pew at church, and on Friday nights in their seats at the high school football game. It was a pretty good life, the kind folk might move to a small city to find.

When people learned that he wore a badge *and* toted a Bible, they usually wanted to know which came first. No question about it. He served God, plain and simple. So far he'd been able to do both, but in the event he couldn't, the resolution was simple. The badge came off.

So how did folks know which job he was doing? He grinned as he remembered how one of his little gray-haired ladies had cleared that up. "It's the hat, Buck. You don't ever wear the hat when you're being a preacher."

She'd been right. He wouldn't wear the hat in church, so he naturally wouldn't wear it when he was praying for someone or teaching about Jesus. But being Sheriff? Well, a guy doesn't look much like a law enforcement officer without the hat, does he? He laughed at the memory, and headed back out the front door, locking it behind him. There'd been an old Clint Eastwood movie where Clint played a prizefighter. When fighting time arrived, the fighter's would turn his hat around backward. It was like throwing a switch.

Buck nodded. Yep. It was that way for him, too. Putting on the hat turned on his sheriff switch, and it helped him make the adjustment.

Most folk would probably be surprised to know he considered the Sheriff's job to be the easy one. Sure, there might actually be some physical danger involved and no doubt a lot of stress, it was pretty clear-cut. People understood what the law was and why a lawman did what he did.

A person's soul on the other hand was a nebulous thing. As a preacher, Buck knew folks weren't always ready to hear what he had to tell them. He figured that carried a whole lot more responsibility.

Chapter 3

Buck poured a cup of coffee and leaned back in his chair. With a grunt he propped his feet up on the middle side drawer of his desk. He didn't like setting them on top. People wandering the hall might think it just a little on the casual side for their sheriff. He could close the door, but he liked to wave at folk walking past, make them feel their sheriff was accessible.

The Sheriff's office was on the ground floor of the courthouse, which occupied a full block in the center of the downtown, across the street from the post office. They shared the facility with other county offices and courtrooms, and the jail occupied the entire top floor.

People invariably loved the cozy, down home feel of Buck's office. He'd given it an old west atmosphere, with a dozen pen and ink sketches of John Wayne and Roy Rogers dotting the walls. Several reproductions of Remington bronzes looked out over the room from various vantage points, and he'd filled one bookcase with a complete set of leather-bound Louis L'Amour western novels. Across the room another bookcase held Biblical tracts and various Christian books. It was a perfect reflection of the two sides of his life.

He sipped the hot coffee, savored the rich aroma that arose from the cup. The tension from the confrontation had begun to slip from him when he stopped at the church, but he realized remnants of adrenaline lingered.

His secretary, Sue, stuck her pretty head in the door. "Sheriff, the state boys called dispatch to let you know there's an abandoned pickup south of town."

He opened his eyes reluctantly, then looked at her without turning his head. He continued to hold the cup in both hands, an inch from his lips. "Why tell me?"

"Because it's Junior Jorgenson's pickup." Junior was a small rancher south of town.

"Doesn't explain why the state boys are calling us. How long did they say it's been there?"

She abandoned the awkward position to move into the doorway. She put her hand on the doorframe and leaned on it. She was a big-boned woman, dark haired, with enough self-confidence to stand up to egos that came natural to the cops that surrounded her all the time. Nodding, she answered. "Penny asked them that. They said it was hard to tell exactly, but they put a red sticker on it when it had been there long enough for them to notice it. They stuck the sticker on about two days ago."

Buck's feet came down with a thump. "Guess we'd better get out there and see about it. Have Charlie Thomas meet us with his wrecker."

She spun on her heel. Standing, he drained off the last of the coffee, then raised his voice slightly. "Sue!"

She had only gotten a couple of steps away. "Yes, sir?"

"Is Raul in there?"

"Yes, sir, he is."

"Tell him I'd like him to go with me, if he isn't tied up."

"I'll do that first."

Buck's chief deputy, Raul, stood six foot five without his boots on and weighed a rock solid 250 pounds. Years ago, when he filled out the job application to join the department, he hadn't classified himself as Hispanic, but instead noted that he had been born and raised in Clear Creek. That said a lot about how he thought of himself, but his features didn't leave his heritage in doubt whether he wrote it on the form or not.

As they drove Raul looked over at the older man. "That was some fracas with the bull dozer."

Buck smiled. "I'll tell you the truth, I was actually a little disappointed that I didn't get to drive it through that house. I know that's no way for a preacher to talk, but ..."

Raul laughed, "Now that's funny, you won't carry a hand gun but you would use a bull dozer on somebody?"

"You're going to get on me about the hand gun again. I don't carry one because it doesn't look right."

"Look right for a preacher or look right for a Sheriff? I just don't believe you have thought it through."

"Like I've told you, my congregation—"

"—knows you are a Sheriff as well as a preacher. They wouldn't think anything about it. But people around town, the image they get is different. You think they believe you could step in and protect them when you don't even carry a gun?"

"I hadn't thought about it like that. Maybe ..."

"Look, it doesn't have to be a big weapon, just something for show." He reached down and took a small holster off his leg, his backup weapon. "Like this Beretta, small and compact, but it'd get the job done in an emergency."

"Maybe you're right. I wouldn't want people to think they couldn't count on me in a pinch."

"Just clip it on your belt where you can get at it."

◊

It took less than ten minutes for them to get out to the flat stretch of highway where the vehicle sat. A state trooper in a gray uniform leaned against the car, his silver beaver cowboy hat rocked back on his head, arms crossed. Sandy Dennis nodded as Buck climbed out of his car. Raul got on the radio to call it in.

Buck acknowledged the tall, good-looking young officer. "Hi, Sandy, you the one who found this thing?"

Sandy leaned forward and offered his hand. "Sure thing, Buck, I first noticed it a couple of days ago and tagged it."

Buck shook his hand. "I'm surprised you found it so quickly. Not a lot of traffic out here. In fact," he shaded his eyes to look down the flat, barren highway, "I'd really hate to head down this thing if I wasn't almighty sure of the wheels under me."

"I know what you mean, Sheriff." Sandy pointed casually down the road. "We patrol this strip at least once a day just in case somebody *is* stranded out here. I mean, you can go a hundred miles on it without seeing a rock, bird or bush, much less meet another car."

"I didn't know you guys hit this stretch so often, but it's a good idea." Buck stepped over to peer into the truck cab, then tried the door. It opened. "It was unlocked when you found it?"

The trooper nodded. "Sure was. I thought I'd wait around for you since your dispatcher said you were on the way."

Buck sat down in the truck, looked into the glove compartment, then over the sun visors.

Raul came over to report on what he had learned on the radio. "We haven't had any reports that included Jorgenson. I called his house on the mobile phone, but didn't get an answer."

Buck pursed his lips, "Thanks. So nothing to tell us why this thing might be sitting out here like this."

The trooper leaned down, arm on the open door, so he could make eye contact. "I don't see any sign of foul play."

"I agree," Buck said. He got out of the truck, hitching his pants up as he did. He glanced over, then reached to open the little door on the gas tank. Inside was a metal key holder with a spare key. "I thought so! I wish people wouldn't do this. They might as well hang a sign on the truck saying PLEASE TAKE ME! Guess we can use it to find out if anything is wrong with the vehicle, though."

He slipped back into the vehicle.

Raul said, "Junior's probably like me. I lock myself out a lot. If I didn't have a spare hidden, I'd be spending half of my time hunting a locksmith. I keep an extra for the front door of my house, too."

Buck stuck the key into the ignition, turned it, and the engine roared to life with a clatter that suggested the oil might need to be checked. "It runs, and the tank is half full of gas. I wonder what the heck is going on?"

Buck shut the engine off and looked at Raul. "Have dispatch cancel the wrecker run, we might as well drive it back in."

"Sure thing." Raul headed back to his unit.

The trooper shook his head. "Can you imagine a vehicle in a big city sitting there for days without being stolen, key or not? I hear tell one can be left for just a few hours, and the owner comes back to find tires and wheels gone, maybe even more."

Buck turned sideways to look at Sandy without craning his neck. "I don't guess you've seen anybody else out here that might have a bearing on this?"

"You know how it is, Sheriff." The trooper moved slightly so his shadow would block the sun from Buck's eyes. "Like I said, there are few cars out here, so you tend to remember the ones you see. You wonder what they're doing and where they're going. Well, actually, I don't wonder so much about the southbound vehicles, but I size up northbound ones to see if I might oughta scare up a reason to stop them. You know, maybe look them over for drugs?"

"Funny you should say that. I was wondering about that very thing earlier. You know, whether we have any sort of drug problem developing? We haven't had any stops that'd be within our jurisdiction, or I'd have heard about it."

"Oh, it's coming through here all right, but we haven't had a lead on anything that'd point to Clear Lake. Wouldn't surprise me though. I expect you'll be seeing more of it. If we snag them inside your county, you can get some nice proceeds from it."

"Yes, I know that." Buck grinned. "Sure would like to see you do more of those stops over this way. Maybe I ought to have my boys work the highway more."

"Wouldn't hurt."

"They'd probably need some training first. I know it requires some probable cause to pull them over."

"Are you kidding me? On 100 miles of road all by myself?" Sandy laughed. "I don't think I ever met anybody out here who wasn't speeding. I just shake a finger at a lot of them, unless they look like somebody I should take a closer look at, or if they're going so fast I simply can't overlook it… or" His grin widened, "…unless I'm just plain bored."

"I'm thinking it could get real boring, riding some of these roads. So tell me, in this case, anything occur to you?"

The trooper glanced at the ground, touched his fingers to his forehead as if it would help him remember, and said, "Only two out here I can think of around then. One was a motor home. I really stopped them to warn them how far it was to another gas station. You know what kind of gas mileage those things get, and it's a long ways to a station that way."

Buck nodded. "And the other?"

"The other was a pumper coming back from his oil lease down south of here."

"You know him?"

"No, but his truck had a Texaco sign on the door."

"Anything else?"

Sandy shook his head. "Like I said, there's not much traffic out here. I'll call you if something comes to mind I've forgotten"

Buck shook his hand. "Thanks a lot, Sandy, I'll let you know what we come up with."

They watched the young trooper drive away. The distinctive black cruiser threw rocks that made Buck half turn in defense, but they missed. "Sorry," Sandy yelled back at him.

Raul walked back over to him. "I caught Charlie, he hadn't even left town."

"Having the only wrecker in town can make a man a mite independent."

"How true."

"Well, this is probably nothing," Buck said.

"Yeah, probably," Raul said.

"Still, if a guy's going to go off and leave his truck sitting around, he generally doesn't leave it out in the middle of nowhere."

"No, that's strange, all right."

"Well, tomorrow we'll start poking around a little and see what we can find." Buck got out of the truck and walked to the patrol car. "You take the truck. I'll take the unit."

"You mean you'll take the air conditioner."

"Now, would I do that?"

Chapter 4

The little town of Clear Creek sat alone in arid West Texas. Technically it was part of the Chihuahuan Desert that extended from this area down into old Mexico. The countryside surrounding the community sat dry and flat, punctuated by low mesquite bushes, which rivaled cactus for the title of the hardiest plants in the world, and by endless lines of pump jacks, which sucked unceasingly at underground pools of oil.

A traffic jam in Clear Creek was not unheard of, but *was* generally of very short duration. Cars would stack up in front of the post office about nine in the morning after the mail had been put up in the boxes. Around Christmas time traffic would get very heavy out by the big discount store and it would get congested downtown right before and after the rodeo parade. Then, of course, Friday nights late in the year, forget about being in a hurry in or out of the football stadium, or for that matter anywhere near it.

One hundred years of cultivation and care had filled Clear Creek with green yards and tree lined roads and parks. The pace of life moved slowly and methodically, characteristic of border communities and their Mexican neighbors. The town doctor lived a few doors down the street, and as Buck got out of his patrol car he saw the rotund little man waddle his way. He leaned back against the car and folded his arms as he awaited Doc's arrival.

Doc puffed and wheezed as he lumbered to a stop. "You're home early today." He reached in his pocket for a handkerchief to mop his face and neck.

"You're a bit early yourself."

"Yeah, I had a tough day." Doc pulled off his hat and wiped the bald spot that glistened above the surrounding white fringe of hair. "That dang fool, Hank Hobart, near took his arm off with a chain saw. I've been working on him for hours."

"Is Hank going to be okay?" Buck's concern was genuine.

"It wasn't life threatening, if that's what you mean. He is going to lose a lot of use of his left hand, I don't know how much. I did my best." He replaced the hat and handkerchief.

"Hank was pretty hard to live with before, he may be plumb impossible now."

"Could go either way. He might find himself more dependent on his wife and treat her better." He frowned. "Are we going to stand out here in the street to talk about this?"

Buck took him by the arm to steer him toward the house. "You're absolutely right, let's go sit down on the porch."

"Might as well." Doc pointed down the sidewalk with a nod of his head, "Here comes Barney."

Buck looked up to see Barney Hoke trudging up the walk. He didn't look much like a scrappy newspaper editor, more like an absent-minded professor. He wore a bow tie and one of his light-colored suits either in the oppressive heat of summer or in the dead of winter – didn't matter to him. His totally gray hair fell over his forehead almost to his dark-rimmed glasses.

They met on the porch, and each helped himself to a drink from the refrigerator Buck kept for the porch-sitting crowd. Barney and the Doc sat down heavily. Buck glanced up at the hooks that held the chains. One of these days that thing simply wasn't going to handle the weight.

This group ended each day sitting right here on the porch.

Barney smiled, "I'm surprised to see you wearing a pistol."

Doc looked surprised, "I hadn't even noticed."

"It's Raul's doing. He convinced me my congregation wouldn't think a thing about it as long as I'm not wearing it at church, and town people might feel like I could actually protect somebody if the situation warranted."

"Well good for him, I've been telling you that for years."

"I guess after that gun play at the shootout it suddenly made sense."

Barney turned his attention to Doc. "I heard you did a nice job on Hank's hand."

Doc shook his head. "I hope so."

Taking a pull on his drink, Barney turned his attention to Buck. "What's this I hear about Junior Jorgenson disappearing?"

"How do you always know so much about what's going on in my office, Barney?" Buck put his feet up on his trashcan. Good footrest, except where he'd cut a hole in the lid to accommodate the beverage cans.

"I'd be a poor newspaperman if I didn't," Barney said, as if that were a complete explanation.

"The highway patrol found his truck abandoned. Raul and I went out to look at it, but we didn't find anything."

"When did they find the truck?"

"A couple of days ago."

Barney said, "He probably only climbed in with someone else, and they went across the border to tie one on. Probably turned into one of those two or three day things."

"Yeah, could be something like that," Buck agreed.

Doc had a different notion. "Yeah, or '*they*' could have come for him." He supplied the quote marks with little scratching motions with two fingers on each hand.

"Who are '*they*'?" Barney mimicked the scratching motions. *Must have smelled an opportunity.*

Doc stuck his nose up in the air slightly. "You know how long Junior has claimed to see UFO's out around his place. He said he's chased the lights a couple of times."

Buck nodded. "He's right there. Junior has filed reports several times. Says he's had some steers butchered, too."

Barney looked down his nose at the two, peering over his glasses like a teacher regarding unruly students. "As I recall, the most plausible theory advanced about that was some sort of satanic rite."

"Yeah, it's true," Buck agreed. "But Junior never believed that explanation. I mean, it ain't like we've got a lot of cult activity around here. Country kids would laugh 'em out of town."

Barney said, "Are you saying you believe this UFO stuff, Buck?"

"Well, no... or maybe. I guess I don't know what I believe as far as UFO's go. There's something going on that ain't been explained to my satisfaction. Some people I know to be honest, truthful folks have sworn they saw some mighty strange stuff. We get quite a few calls on it."

Buck looked down as he weighed what it all meant before he

added, "Reckon I'm not ready to say I believe, but there's way too much which don't add up. I guess I'm still open to more information on the subject."

Barney shook his head. "I might buy such an attitude from a sheriff, Buck, but from a preacher, I find it another thing entirely."

Buck's head came up. "Why would my being a minister make a difference?"

"Well, I think… actually, I guess it's because… oh, I don't know, Buck, it just seems like it should. The Bible doesn't say anything about people being created anywhere else, just on earth."

"No, that's true, but it doesn't say they weren't created elsewhere either. This is a mighty big universe."

Barney's mouth hung open, "You believe that?"

"I told you I don't know what I believe when it comes to that. God's big enough to do it if he wants to. I guess down deep I think if he'd made people somewhere else he would have mentioned it to the folks he used to write the Bible. Who knows? I don't claim to know the mind of God."

Barney snickered, "I can't tell whether it's the lawman or the preacher that won't take a side on it. Actually, I suppose I don't understand how you can wear a badge and tote a Bible at the same time."

Doc said, "That's like asking whether it's the Democrats or the Republicans that won't let it rain."

Barney rose to the bait. "No, I know the answer to that one, it's them dang Democrats."

That set it off, but the banter didn't divert Buck's attention from the question, "Which one is it you think I'm not getting done,

Barney?"

"You seem to be doing both real well," Barney cleared his throat and shifted position on the swing "You want us to run a story on Junior's disappearance?"

"Couldn't hurt. You might say we're looking for more information on the abandoned pickup. Maybe somebody will call in."

Barney pulled a small notebook from his shirt pocket and made a notation on it. "Okay, long as I have your permission to go with it." After a couple of instances in the past, a rule had been adopted that anything said on the porch, *stayed* on the porch unless permission was specifically given to use it.

Raul pulled his unit up to the curb out front. Charley Little Bear, Buck's oldest friend, got out of the passenger side. A full blood Navajo Indian, Little Bear wore his dark black hair caught up in two braids that fell below his shoulders, and his black, flat-brimmed hat sported a very colorful beaded hatband. He was even shorter than Buck, but significantly outweighed him.

Buck held up his hands in a questioning gesture. "Somebody call a meeting?"

Raul said, "Thought I'd stop by and tell you I drove by Junior's house. Still no sign he's been around."

"That bothering you?"

Raul frowned, "It's not like Junior to go off and leave his truck that way."

"Well, you boys pull up a chair, and we'll see if we can make some sense of it." Buck jerked a thumb toward the refrigerator. "Get you something to drink."

Chapter 5

When Buck arrived at his office the following morning, he and Raul prepared to go over some paperwork. Before he sat down at his desk, Buck stopped to look out of the window.

"What are you watching?" Raul asked.

"Mrs. McAbee's headed to the post office."

The big deputy came up beside him. "Let me see."

Mrs. McAbee was somewhere in her upper 80's. She had a total disregard of stop signs or objects such as cars, trucks, or pedestrians when she drove. The entire community knew Mrs. McAbee had the right-of-way, and everybody actively dodged her. It had become something of a game, even a community amusement. It wasn't particularly difficult as her car seldom rolled faster than 15 miles per hour.

They could barely see her tiny white head through the window of the big vehicle. It was the perfect car for her, a 1940 Chevy coupe, the American automotive world's equivalent of the Sherman tank.

It had stood up to the catastrophes of her driving with little more than scratches or scrapes.

Buck pointed and said, "Homer better quit reading his mail and pay attention to where he's going." Homer was a scarecrow of a man, and ran the five and dime downtown.

"Or more appropriately pay attention to where *she* is going, else she may get him this time."

"She got him last August. It ought to be somebody else's turn." Buck released the catch on the window to swing it out, ready to call down to Homer.

Raul smiled. "Oh, good, he saw her."

"Looks like it." Buck shook his head as he secured the latch again. "But Mrs. Goodson is backing out, and Mrs. McAbee doesn't see her."

They both clenched their teeth. "Who-o-o-o-oa! Man, that was close."

"Well, we're safe for now, she's pulling into a parking space."

"Yeah, and clear up on the curb."

Buck laughed. "And nearly got Homer... again."

"When are we going to ask the state to pull her license?"

Buck turned from the window, eased himself back into the comfortable wooden office chair. "I've talked to folks about it, and I can't find anybody who wants us to do it. Everybody seems to think she's an institution. I'll be retiring soon, and you can do it then."

Raul smiled as he sat down in the chair that faced Buck's desk. "No, I guess you're right. The town really wouldn't be the same without Mrs. McAbee."

Their diversion ended, they dove into the stack of reports on the desk and stayed with it for several hours. Finally, Buck pushed back and said, "I've had about all of this I can enjoy in one sitting. How about we go out and check to see if Junior's come home yet?"

"Don't have to ask me twice." Raul reached for his hat.

Junior's house was a small, two-bedroom, wood-frame structure, as unassuming as the little ranch itself. As they pulled into the yard, they saw Junior's ranch hand feeding the horses. Raul said, "His name is Jack Dulaney, right?"

"Yeah, I know Jack."

Jack was a splinter of a man, and he hefted a hay bale with as much difficulty as a person might expect of a man nearing seventy.

They stepped out of the car and Raul said, "Hey Jack, you shouldn't be doing such heavy work at your age."

"When I can't get the job done, I'll quit." The cowboy's tone was brusque, but not unfriendly. He wiped his forehead with his shirtsleeve.

"Didn't mean to suggest you couldn't, but I would think you'd rate a little easier lifestyle by now. You've paid your dues."

Jack pulled off the heavy leather gloves to tuck them in his back pocket and sat down on the bales. "It's all I know… wouldn't know how to live any other way."

Raul nodded. "Is Junior around?"

The old man shook his head. "Ain't seen him for a couple of days. He's off somewhere in his pickup, though, 'cause it ain't here."

Buck came around the car. "We found the truck out on the highway, Jack, but Junior wasn't with it. The truck is down at the office now."

The ranch hand seemed genuinely surprised. He pushed his hat back on his head. "You don't say! That don't make no sense. Why in tarnation would he go off and leave his truck?"

"We were hoping you could tell us." Buck studied the man.

All he saw was concern, or maybe puzzlement. On Jack's face it was hard to tell.

"Maybe it was out of gas."

"No, we found the spare key and drove it in. Had a half tank of gas."

"I'll be dogged." Jack took his hat off to scratch his head as if it would make an answer come to mind.

Raul asked the obvious question. "It's not like him to go off like this?"

"Naw, he don't ever go off without making sure I know to feed the stock." Jack put his hat back on, tugged it firmly into place. .

"Looks to me like you know to do it anyway." Buck put one foot up on a hay bale, then leaned forward to rest an elbow on his knee.

"Sure I do, and he knows it, but you know how it is. It makes a man feel easier in his mind to be sure he's covered it. That's why it's funny, him going off without saying anything."

"I understand," Buck said. "Listen, has he got a hideout key to his house around here?"

"Sure thing, under the big flower pot on the porch. He don't ever lock it though."

Buck took his foot down and started in that direction. "Guess we'll take a look around," he said over his shoulder. "See if there's anything that might tell us what's going on." He looked back. "You better come with us, if you don't mind. You might spot something we'd miss."

Jack didn't answer, but fell in behind them. The house was a typical bachelor domicile, relatively neat, but not clean. Buck figured most women might find it amusing, and most mothers would be horrified, but a dusty house was a real bonus to an investigator. One could literally date the last time anything had been touched by the amount of dust on it. And if something were missing, it'd be sure to leave a clean imprint where it had stood.

They looked the place over carefully, but failed to find anything useful. They were on their way back out to the patrol unit when a call came over the radio on Raul's utility belt. They looked at each other as the electronic voice announced an inmate had escaped from the county jail.

Chapter 6

Buck pulled the cellular phone out of the holder on his belt, while Raul slid behind the wheel. "Dispatch, this is the sheriff."

"Yes sir?

"Raul and I are on our way in. We need to get units out on the four roads leading out of town. Seal it off. Check all outbound vehicles, then see if we can get the state boys to take over that chore so we can have more units to search around town. Got it?" Buck continued to stand with his hand on the door as he issued orders.

"Yes, sir," said the voice.

"Make sure everybody knows who we're looking for."

"Yes, sir."

"One more thing."

"What's that, Sheriff?"

"Just who are we looking for?"

There was a muffled laugh. "It's Ruben Garcia, Sheriff."

"Garcia? Wasn't he one of the trustees doing painting around the courthouse?"

"Yes, sir."

"Well, get those roads sealed off. We're on our way back in."

He punched the button to hang up the phone, sat down in the car and looked over at Raul. "Let's go," he said. "And tell me again what Garcia was in for."

Raul lit up the beacons and squealed tires on the driveway before he answered. "He was set to go to trial next week for allegedly raping his former wife. He's been in the state pen at Huntsville for a parole violation, but he was brought back for this trial."

Buck chewed on this information as he clutched the dashboard. He hoped the lights and siren would clear the intersections Raul was roaring through. He forced his mind back on the subject.

"What made us think he was no risk of flight?"

"We didn't think any such thing, Sheriff," the big man objected. "Seeing as he had no history of violence, he was one of the trustees doing a little light work around the place. That didn't mean he wasn't locked up, just wasn't confined in a cell."

"We'll need to re-evaluate that decision process," Buck said with a scowl. "In the meantime, do we have anything on friends or relatives?"

"I'll check on it first thing," Raul pulled into the courthouse parking lot. Raul headed off to fulfill his mission, and Buck climbed the stairs to the jail.

He walked in to find a lock down in effect. The jailer, Jim Jackson, flushed a deep red when he saw Buck approach. Whether he was at fault or not, jailers took this kind of thing very personally.

"What you got there, Jim?" Buck indicated the object in Jim's hands with a nod of his head.

"It's a homemade rope, Sheriff. Garcia made it out of sheets and painter's cloth. He even reinforced it with masking tape."

Buck inspected the rope with a grimace. "I'm sure glad we provided him with everything he needed. How'd he get out?"

"He got out this window over here," the jailer led the way. "Garcia was painting this hallway and used the activity for cover while he picked the lock on this window. You see this expandable metal cover opens up when the lock is open." He opened the window to demonstrate.

He secured the window again before he continued, "He waited until we were busy getting the meals up, Sheriff, then he kicked out the window and went down the rope. We saw the break as soon as we came in with the meals. We alerted everyone downstairs, but there was no sign of him."

"I see."

"They did turn up one witness who said she saw some guy in jail coveralls get into a car. She said it was a tan colored station wagon, and she thought the car had two females in it, but she didn't get much of a look at them."

The phone rang, and the jailer picked it up. He shook his head. "Okay, I'll tell him." Hanging up the phone, he said, "Sheriff, you've got press downstairs."

"Locals?"

"TV guys, too."

"So fast? I hate those silly helicopters. Used to be, they couldn't get here in time to bug us."

He had but a few minutes to compose his thoughts on the way down the stairs. He knew what the questions would be. The lights came on as he hit the bottom step and microphones poked out toward him. Regardless of how they were worded, he managed to work in the response he wanted to make as he fielded the questions.

Yelling to be heard above the rest, a reporter asked, "Sheriff, can you tell us how the prisoner escaped?"

"The prisoner's name is Ruben Garcia, and he's a trustee, which means he was out doing light work around the facility."

"You mean he was out running loose?" another reporter asked.

Trust these guys to word everything in the most negative context. "The inmate was low-security with no history of violence, so he's no threat to the community. He compromised the security on a back window while we were busy fixing their meal to make his escape."

"Sheriff, how did he get out the window? That's on the third floor?" the first reporter asked.

"He made a rope out of his sheets and the drop cloths he was using to paint with."

"What are you doing to find him?"

"The whole department is on the job, backed by the State Department of Public Safety, the Texas Rangers, and personnel from the state prison. Those people are trained for exactly this sort of situation. There's nothing to be concerned about. The inmate will be back in custody within a very short period of time."

He waved off additional questions and added, "People need to realize there has never been any cause for us to question jail procedures, they've always been adequate in the past.. However, I assure you that policies and procedures will be reviewed for needed changes."

"Whose fault is this, Sheriff?"

"The jailer has the ultimate responsibility upstairs, but like President Truman said, the buck stops here, no pun intended. I'm not pointing any fingers, so, if you'll excuse me, we have to go catch this guy." Sure, he could have hung the jailer out to dry, but he didn't work that way. He stood by his people.

Back in the office, Raul said, "Nice work."

"I didn't exactly dazzle them with my footwork, but maybe I got it done."

"Looked like it to me."

Buck sat on the edge of a desk, "So, where are we?"

"Roadblocks are out. The DPS relieved us on the two checkpoints out on the Interstate. The Rangers sealed the private airport and checked out the bus station. Carol and Mike stopped the only train on its way out of town and searched it before they let it leave. Frank took his plane up and did a 360 degree search to insure Garcia wasn't hoofing it out of town across open country."

"Good... good... he's still in town then, unless he dug out like a gopher. Send someone up with Frank with a video-cam to search by air. Ask them to cover all the territory they can with the cameras, then bring me the tape. Maybe the long lens will spot something eyeballs aren't seeing."

Raul turned to go. Buck stopped him. "Wait a minute. Before you leave, did you get anything on friends or relatives?"

Raul jerked a thumb back over his shoulder. "I was just about to tell you, his former wife is in the squad room."

"The one he's in jail for raping?"

"The one he's *accused* of raping."

Buck got up. "Right, my mistake. How come she's here so

quick?"

"We called her first thing. Thought she might be in some danger. I told her we'd send somebody out for her, but instead she hotfooted it right down here. She felt it was safer to be here."

"I take it, we still sent somebody out to the house?"

"Absolutely. Bill is there, but I had him dropped off so there wouldn't be a patrol unit sitting outside."

"Good thinking. Did she give us a lead on anybody else?"

"She just now got here, boss. I haven't had time to talk to her yet."

"Okay, go send somebody up with Frank. I'll deal with her."

Buck walked into the squad room to find a short, but very pretty lady. She had smooth walnut-colored skin, with a ready smile that dazzled when she turned it on, as she did now. She swiveled toward him in the desk chair and fidgeted nervously with her handbag. He said, "Ms. Garcia?"

"It's Gonzales, Sheriff. I asked for my maiden name back in the divorce."

"I'm sorry, I should have found that out before I came in."

"No need to apologize. It's a natural mistake."

Buck perched on the edge of the desk by her. "Well then, Ms. Gonzales, can you give us any idea where Garcia may have gone?"

"He only had a couple of friends at most who might stand up for him. I gave their names to your deputy, and he went off to check on them." She punctuated the sentence with a perfunctory wave in the direction Raul had gone.

"Not by himself, I hope," he looked the question over to the dispatcher.

"Mike and Carol are meeting him," Penny said.

"Good." His attention returned to the woman. "A witness said she saw him get into a station wagon with a couple of females. Mean anything to you?"

"It means I did the right thing divorcing him. He always had some bimbo on the side. I don't know who the latest one is."

"You really think he might have come looking for you?"

"My testimony is sure to add to his jail time."

Buck looked at the prisoner's file. "This says he had no history of violence. It doesn't sound like something that would fit with a rape charge."

"I guess it means he never beat or abused me. The only force he ever used was to hold me down while he had his way with me. He never recognized my right to say no. Not while we were married or even after."

Buck shook his head, "I surely don't understand such people."

"Join the club, Sheriff."

Chapter 7

The radio crackled as Carol's voice came on the air. "This is unit four."

Buck stepped over to the dispatcher to pick up the microphone. "This is unit one, go ahead."

"Sheriff, we have both suspects from the getaway vehicle here, but they claim they haven't seen him and don't know a thing. They gave us permission to search, but we didn't turn anything up."

"Tell them I'd like to have a little visit, but I'm a little busy now. We'd better make it tomorrow."

Before he had time to turn away from the radio, he heard Raul's voice. "Sheriff? You still there?"

"Whatcha got, Raul?"

"I've been visiting with an informer we've used occasionally. He told me to go check on an abandoned house over on Fourth Street."

"What number?"

"901."

"Meet you there in ten minutes." He set the mike down, poised a moment, deep in thought. "Penny, have a unit back them up. Tell them to approach the location from the rear."

He turned back to Mrs. Gonzales, removing his hat. "Ma'am, I'm sorry to run out on you, but—"

"It's all right, Sheriff. If you don't mind, I think I'll stick around here for a bit yet."

"Yes, ma'am, I understand. I think we'll be relieving your mind here very shortly."

Raul was standing by his unit as Buck drove up, but he leaned in, got his riot gun, and handed it to the sheriff.

Buck worked the pump on the weapon. "You seen any signs of life?"

"Not while I've been here."

The radio hissed, "Unit two, unit five is in position to back you up now."

Raul acknowledged. "This is unit two, be advised the Sheriff has assumed tactical command."

"Does this remind you of that little shoot-out we had the other day?"

"Does that mean you're going to threaten to level the house with a bulldozer again?" Raul said with a grin.

"Not unless I have to, but there's no telling what kind of weapon he may have had time to get. I don't want anybody getting hurt, especially me." He picked up the microphone and turned the switch to PA."

"Attention in the house, Ruben, this is Sheriff Green. We've got the place completely covered. If we have to come in and look for you, we're going to be very trigger-happy, if you know what I mean."

They waited for several minutes with no response. Lights came on all over the neighborhood, and people came out into their yards.

Buck grimaced at Raul. "Great. Another chance to look like a first class jerk if this guy isn't in there." He keyed the mike again. "You people get back in your houses. We may be about to open fire on this house, and I don't want anybody getting hit by a stray bullet."

Raul suppressed a smile. "You talking to those folks or to Garcia?"

"Both."

"Sheriff?" the radio said.

"Go ahead."

"Somebody just crawled out from under a bed in this back bedroom. I've got him in my sights."

"Cover him, but don't shoot unless I give the word."

A voice came from the house. "Hold your fire, I'm coming out."

Buck picked up the microphone again. "If you've got a weapon, throw it out first."

A knife clattered down the walk. It looked like a big kitchen knife. The deputies moved to take him into custody.

Garcia stepped out with his hands in the air. He was still wearing the bright orange jail coveralls. He had a nervous little smile on his face underneath a little pencil mustache.

A deputy moved up behind him and put him on his face, quickly patting him down and snapping handcuffs on his wrists.

"That it?" Buck said, "Only a knife?"

"Nothing else, Sheriff, he's clean," a deputy said.

"Okay, take him back to jail, boys." Buck saw Doc and Barney standing a few steps away. "Sorry about the timing on this, Barney."

"Sorry?" Doc gave him a quizzical look.

Barney smiled. "Our good sheriff knows the capture came after we put the paper to bed. He's saying that he is aware that it favors the electronic guys."

"Oh, I see."

"Don't worry, Doc. Much as we'd like to be able to break all of the news first, we know we have a limited window each day. However, the good part is most people read us for details even if they've already heard it first somewhere else."

Buck smiled, "And I can't tell you how glad I am you feel that way, Barney."

"Well, you guys did a good job rounding the escapee up so quickly."

"Thanks. Is it what you're gonna say in the paper?"

"Front page."

Doc said, "How about Junior? Anything turn up on him?"

"Every time I try to get to work on it I get sidetracked, Doc. We'll get back on it in the morning."

Chapter 8

"Like my mother used to say, what if your face froze like that?"

Buck looked up to find Raul waiting in the open doorway. "Like what?"

Raul leaned against the doorframe. "I'm not sure I know what the expression you're wearing means... puzzled, maybe?"

"Yeah, for sure I'd say puzzled." Buck pushed back in his chair.

"By what?"

He nodded toward the small TV combo video player sitting on his desk "This video tape they brought back from the fly over."

"What do we need that for? Garcia's back in jail."

"I just thought I'd look at it, particularly at the area over by Junior's place."

"Good idea, I wouldn't have thought of it. See anything?"

"I'm not sure. Take a look at this." Raul came around the desk as Buck triggered the remote.

"See all those tire tracks going back there?" He pointed, "Now it's going to come up closer in a minute or so."

They watched as the camera panned back further, then Buck pressed the pause button. "Now... look there... Those tracks come over here, then they turn around and go back. And look at these tracks up and down this little section here."

Raul looked closely, "If I didn't know better, I'd say it looks like a small plane has been landing."

"Exactly what it looks like to me, too, only I've been sitting here wondering why." Buck leaned back in his chair, swiveling to face the big man. "The first thing that comes to mind is drugs, of course, particularly after the mess we just finished with. What I'm thinking about now is whether I can come up with some less ominous reasons."

Raul sat in the chair by the desk. "Buck, you know lots of ranchers out here fly their own planes. So does the guy over at the insurance office."

"But Junior doesn't fly a plane."

"A lot of his friends do. Maybe they picked him up and went hunting, or they went to Dallas together."

Buck steepled his fingers giving it further thought. "But if that was the case, why was his truck way over on the highway?"

Raul shook his head. "You got me there. One good thing, though."

"What's that?"

"Doc's UFO's wouldn't leave those kind of track marks."

Buck leaned forward, "How do you know? You ever seen where one landed?"

Raul grinned. "No, I guess I wouldn't know a UFO landing site if it up and bit me."

Buck's secretary came in. "Sheriff, Garcia has a couple of visitors. Two young girls."

"All right, let them finish their visit then bring them in. In the meantime, Raul, get their names from the log and see if you can get an ID on them."

About ten minutes later, Carol ushered the two girls into the office. Buck stood and motioned them and Carol to a chair. It was policy always to have a female officer present with a female in the office, particularly juveniles. "Carol, do you mind introducing me?"

"This is Debbye Sanchez, and that's Sonora McCall."

"McCall?"

The young girl flushed, "My father is an Anglo, Sheriff." Her light skin and features supported the statement, although her Hispanic heritage was still quite evident. Both girls were attractive, but both wore entirely too much makeup.

"I see, well, my name is Buck Green, and I'm glad to meet you ladies."

"Are we in trouble?" Debbye asked.

"What makes you think you might be?"

They looked at each other but apparently decided not to answer.

"Cat got your tongue, huh?" He sat down. "Well, let me see if I can do something with this. Yes, you could be in very serious trouble. Ordinarily I might advise you to call your parents and maybe even have them call an attorney. However, we may can keep it from being such a big deal."

He looked at the two girls, still no response. "I do want to tell you if you start getting worried at any time you can stop this little discussion and call your parents. If you do, however, things will then become official and go on the record. For right now, we're only talking. You understand what I'm saying?"

Both girls nodded almost imperceptivity to indicate they did.

Raul came in the door, and Buck looked over to him. "The girls are here in a tan 1987 Ford station wagon, Sheriff."

"I thought that might be the case." Looking back at the girls, he added, "Do you girls know why we find this small fact interesting?"

They shook their head in unison.

"Oh, I think you do. A witness saw Ruben Garcia climb into a tan station wagon and drive away from the courthouse. The same witness said she thought there were two females in the car."

"Sheriff," Debbye said, "I think I had better make the call to my parents now."

"Me, too," Sonora said.

Buck pushed the phone toward them on his desk. "Your choice, but remember, this becomes official when they get involved. You will be charged with aiding and abetting. Do you know what that is?"

They nodded.

"If you want to talk a little further, perhaps we can keep anything from going on the record. I'll give you my word before anything official happens, your parents will be present, and you don't have to answer anything you don't want to."

"All right, Sheriff," Debbye said reluctantly. "We'll wait for a few minutes."

"I'm not going to ask you to confirm helping Garcia, because that would make things official right off. *If* you did so, however, it was very foolish to come visit him the next day and in the same car."

Debbye suddenly sat forward in her chair. "We didn't intend

to be involved, Sheriff. We only came to visit him yesterday, but as we pulled up, he came running across the lawn and jumped in."

"I thought it might be something like that. Why were you involved with him in the first place?"

"To get a recording contract," Debbye hung her head.

Buck fought to hide a small smile. "And you think he could get you one?"

Sonora jumped in, her voice animated. "Sure, he's the vice president of a Tejano music label."

"How do you know that?"

"He told us... and he gave us his card."

Buck held a hand, palm up toward them. "I could get a card printed that said I was the President of the United States, but it wouldn't make it so. But let me ask you this, how did he explain being in jail?"

"He said it was a technicality, a copyright infringement."

This time he couldn't keep from laughing. "And you believed that? Did he come across with a recording session?"

Sonora's lower lip showed Buck's laugh had impacted her. "Not yet, he wanted to see if we knew how the game was played first."

"The game?"

Debbye said, "Sure, Sheriff, we're not babies. We understand you have to play ball to get anywhere in the recording industry."

"And did you play ball?"

They both blushed an incredible shade of red. "Well... Yes."

Buck could only shake his head.

Debbye added, "Ruben, that is, Mr. Garcia, just had to make

sure we knew the facts of life about the business. He needed to know we were tough enough to make it."

"Well, now that he's acquainted you with the facts of life, I'm going to finish the job." He looked at Raul and told him to go call their parents. "Okay, first, I'm not going to charge you with aiding and abetting, at least not yet. But I don't want you to think you've gotten away with anything. I'm going to put all of the information necessary to pursue the case in a file, nice and handy. If you keep your noses clean, we won't need the file and nobody will ever know. Other than your parents, that is."

The girls looked relieved. Relieved wasn't the reaction he wanted.

"Now, hang on to your seats, because here comes the real truth." He leaned forward on the desk. "Ruben has been in jail, not working at some record company. He used you, and he took advantage of you, and we intend to add those charges to the ones he's already facing. That's for starters. Next, I'm sure there is some hanky-panky going on in the record industry, there always has been. But I seriously doubt anybody with half a brain is trying it on jail-bait girls."

He got up and went around the desk, closer to them. "You wanted to prove you weren't babies, and you knew what was going on? Well, you proved exactly the opposite. You proved you don't have enough sense to go running around unsupervised."

He went back to his chair. "You'll find the conditions of my not filing these charges will require you to be closely supervised. I'm going to insist your parents ground you, allow you to go to school, to church and, to your home. And just in case you can get around them, which you probably can, I'm going to have my deputies stay on the lookout for you. If they spot you out, they'll be asking if you have your parents' permission to be there. We'll want to know who you will be with, where you are going, and when you will return. They may even follow up to check that you're where you said you will be."

Sonora blubbered, "You... you... you can't do this. It's worse than going to jail."

"If you don't like it, you can complain, and I'll go ahead with the formal charges. It's your choice."

"What would happen if we did?" Debbye asked.

Buck held up a hand, then let it fall. "At the very least, you would go straight to juvenile detention to be held until you reach your majority, at which time you would be tried as an adult for aiding the escape of a felon. My way might seem harsh for the short term, but it gives you a chance to escape without a criminal record."

Both girls were crying, but had nothing further to say. Carol led them out to wait for their parents.

Raul said, "You were rough on them."

Buck nodded. "I know, but I can't let them go off thinking this was a lark. They need to pay the price, but I don't want it to be a price that'll ruin the rest of their lives. Of course, it's gonna come out to a degree when they have to testify at his trial."

"You're going to charge him for what he did with minors?"

"Does a bear live in the woods? Of course, I'm going to charge him."

Raul smiled. "Good, I was hoping you would. You know

you're exceeding your authority on most of those conditions you set on the girls."

"I would be if I were doing it officially. I'm asking them and their parents to cooperate voluntarily to keep me from taking official action. They can always refuse."

"Like they would be dumb enough to do that."

"Precisely." He gave Raul a crooked smile. "Besides, a tragedy like this will be a major topic of conversation over at the school. I think it'll be a whale of an object lesson. I do intend deputies to check on them periodically for a while and make their lives interesting, then we'll work out some way for them to earn their way out of it."

"That has to be the oldest come-on in the books. I can't believe those girls went for it."

"Fame and fortune, Raul, fame and fortune. Young girls just can't see when they have stars in their eyes. If some young stud hit on them, they'd see through it in a minute, but when the stars get in their eyes... "

They sat in silence for a couple of minutes before Buck changed the subject. "Getting back to business, how about getting hold of Little Bear for me? Ask him if he can go out with me to check out those tracks at Jorgenson's place."

"Good idea, he can read the ground like we read the newspaper. What time?"

"Tell him to figure on the first thing in the morning."

Chapter 9

To Little Bear, in the morning meant at first light. Buck wasn't surprised to see him when the sun was barely up. Buck poured a couple of travel mugs full of coffee before they headed out in his cruiser. It was full light by the time they reached Junior Jorgenson's place. Buck started to drive into the area he'd been interested in on the videotape, but Little Bear stopped him. "Is Junior's hired hand the only other one around here?"

"His name is Jack Dulaney. That's him over by the barn."

Jack waved and started toward them. Buck introduced them and told Jack what they were doing. While Buck was speaking, Little Bear squatted down, looking at Jack's footprints.

Jack gave him a questioning look, and Little Bear said, "I need to be able to read the ground. Now I know your prints when I see them. Is there any place where there are prints you know for sure to be those of Junior?"

"In the garden. Nobody messes with the garden but Junior."

Buck said, "Well, you ought to mess with it. You'd better get a little water on it, or it's going to be toast by the time Junior comes back."

Jack nodded and went after a hose.

Little Bear poked among the plants for a few minutes. "I have him now, let me see if I can find anyone else," he said when he got back.

Over near the house he recognized Buck and Raul's footprints but not the two other sets of prints. He pointed them out. "Expensive dress shoes. I would say new and from the point of the toe, probably Italian. They went one time in and one time out."

"Is he kidding?" Jack asked. He was standing there holding a rolled hose.

"Not a smidgen, I'm surprised he didn't give us the brand name of the shoes." Turning back to Little Bear, Buck said, "What can you tell me about the guys wearing them?"

"Good-sized men, if they have average feet for their size. That would make both maybe six feet tall and close to 200 pounds. This guy," he pointed to a track, "was carrying a briefcase or suitcase. It was heavier going out than it was coming in. I'd say the tracks are a couple of weeks old."

"I'm not believing this," Jack said.

"Put your money up." Buck grinned.

The hired man faced the Indian. "How could you possibly know all of that just from some old tracks?"

"My friend, I haven't gotten to the hard part yet." He had only the faintest trace of a smile on his dark face. "The shape of the shoes says Italian, and the unmarked soles says new. A lot of years tracking tells me how to determine their size from the print, unless they have above or below average size feet. This happens less than 20 percent of the time.

"I got the weight by comparing the depth of the track to our own. The difference in depth on one side told me of the suitcase and the change in weight going in and coming out. I can determine the age of the prints because the tracks disappear as they get out to where the wind can disperse them. Also, the little rain we had a couple of weeks ago affected them. Those prints were here before the marks of the shower."

"That's amazing!"

Little Bear shrugged, "Elementary, my dear Watson."

"What?" Jack said.

"It's from a book."

"Wait until you see him get warmed up," Buck added.

Jack walked up with a hose. "All right if I water now?" Jack asked.

"How about if you put it on slow and drive out with us while it waters?"

On the way Buck explained what he had seen on the videotape. Little Bear stopped Buck short of his destination. "Please wait here until I wave you in, I need to walk it first before we make any new prints."

By the time he waved Buck and Jack in, he had worked the prints out. He was squatting, poking at a track with a small twig when they joined him. He pointed with a nod of his head. "One vehicle, with passenger car tires, met a plane. The same three sets of tracks we found at the house are here, Junior and the two strangers, and the age looks to be the same, a couple of weeks ago. From the looks of the ground, there are lots of old tracks underneath. People have met a plane here, probably more than once."

Buck turned to look at the ranch hand. "You seen anybody around of that description?"

"No, but we do have a plane land here occasionally. I ain't

never seen anybody connected with it. I seem to always be working someplace way off when it happens."

Buck shook his head, "How convenient. Sounds more and more like drugs, doesn't it?"

Jack got a skeptical look on his face. "Drugs? No way, not Junior."

The Navajo nodded. "I figure Junior met someone over on the highway and got in with them. They stopped at his house and put something into a suitcase. Then they came out here to meet the plane."

"Junior got in, too?" Buck asked.

Little Bear got to his feet indicating the tracks in front of him with sweeping gesture of an open hand. "I can't find any place where he stepped on top of their tracks. The fact that he didn't, either here or at the house, doesn't rule out him being either place after they left. But it does mean there is no evidence he was here following their departure."

"Let's get this clear," Buck said, "are you saying you're sure he got on the plane?"

"They're walking on each other's tracks here. He could have gotten on the plane, or he could have gotten back in this car. I'm fairly sure he did not go back into his house."

"Well, it sounds like we had the suspects from the other drug deal in jail before these tracks were made, so if it's drugs, it's a whole different thing. What do you think?"

"I read tracks, Buck, not minds."

They dropped Jack back at the ranch and Little Bear back at his car before returning to the office. There Buck briefed Raul on what they had discovered.

Raul said, "You figure they stopped at Junior's house to get money?"

"I don't know what else it could be. I think maybe they met this plane and traded money for something. Drugs is the most likely bet. I can't think of anything else that fits the facts right now. But I gotta say I never figured Junior for anything like that."

Raul agreed. "Makes sense to me, I can't think of anything people smuggle *out* of the country. Junior certainly didn't make it back to his truck. But I agree, doesn't seem like something Junior would be involved in."

"No, and it doesn't seem to give us any kind of loose end to follow." Buck thought on it for a minute, then said, "Let's try this. Have our people check the motels, restaurants, and service stations, see if they served a couple of big guys in expensive shoes, which probably means expensive clothes, from about a month ago. They ought to stick out right considerable among all of the boots and jeans around here. Maybe somebody will remember something."

Raul started for the door. "We'll get right on it."

Raul almost collided with the dispatcher on his way out. He stepped back to see what she had for them. "There's a call out at the fairgrounds. There's been a series of car break-in's, mostly radios and CD players."

"Get a unit out there. I don't suppose there are any witnesses or anything?"

Penny smiled. "Even better. They said they have the perpetrator trapped."

"Trapped… where?"

"They said you really need to come see."

Raul said, "I better go with you."

It only took a few minutes to get over to the fairgrounds. A crowd stood around a small motor home, gaping at a middle-aged man who lay on the floorboard with a large black Doberman perched on the seat above him.

Raul said, "Sheriff's department! Come out of there!"

The man started to comply when suddenly the docile Doberman became all teeth and snarling fury. The man stiffened, and the dog eased back, calm and contented.

"Well if that don't beat all." Buck pushed his hat back on his head. Looking around, he said loudly, "Is the owner of this animal here?"

An elderly man with dark hair and sideburns stepped forward. "I'm the one who called, Officer. I'm Tony Carnahan." Looking at the dog, he said, "Sugar, you may go back and lay down now. You've done very well."

The dog jumped from the seat and went back to lie down under the table. A deputy stepped forward and took the man into custody.

"You see," he continued, "Sugar is trained to not bark when someone disturbs the vehicle. She allows him to break in, then once the intruder is on the floorboard or back in the vehicle where she can get between him and the door, then she turns into the 'Dog from Hell.' Convincing, wouldn't you say?"

"It'd do it for me," Raul agreed.

"Actually, she's very sweet when she isn't doing her thing. This, gentlemen, is Sugar's fifth capture, the second one this year."

"Does she testify against them in court, too?"

Carnahan allowed himself a slight smile. "You're being facetious, of course, but were she to be asked to do it, I have no doubt she could pick her man out of a lineup."

Buck reached back in his unit and came out with one of the plastic courtesy badges he used as a memento for kids and visitors. "Well, pin this on her collar. She's an official Clear Creek deputy now, authorized to make arrests in my jurisdiction. Actually, I'd like to have her in my department full time."

Carnahan smiled again, "Yes, I'm sure she would do well, but I'm afraid I can't get along without her." He called the dog to him and started to put the badge on her.

Buck raised his brows as he saw there were already badges there. "Where'd those others come from?"

"New York and Houston."

"Well, hold off with that one. We can't let them big city boys upstage us." He called the office and had a deputy run out one of the small gold-plated badges worn by members of the Sheriff's Posse.

When Carol brought the badge, she and Raul stood at attention while Buck pinned it on.

Sugar cocked her head and looked for all the world as if she were smiling.

Chapter 10

A pretty good congregation showed up for Wednesday night services. Buck looked out over his small sanctuary from the small platform with the pulpit on it, to the rows of benches that would only hold a couple hundred people at capacity.

Doc was there, of course. Somehow it didn't seem right that he had a better attendance record as an agnostic than some of Buck's most devout members. Doc would be putting his rebuttal material together to give Buck a hard time about the message later.

Buck couldn't help but wonder if Doc wasn't really a closet Christian, who only professed to be a non-believer to make him jump through the hoops. If that was true, it was working.

Buck kicked things off with, "I'm taking my text tonight from Leviticus 19, verse 18: 'Thou shalt not avenge, nor bear any grudge against the children of thy people, but thou shalt love thy neighbor as thyself: I am the LORD.'"

He gazed out over the congregation. "I don't suppose I have to explain why I'm preaching on this passage. There isn't much loving thy neighbor taking place in town these days."

Some of the ranch people looked at each other as if they thought he'd lost his mind.

He saw the looks and continued. "Maybe you folks who live out of town aren't caught up in this, but if that's the case, before you go back to the ranch today, you'll see." Leafing through the text, he said, "Turn to Matthew 12, verse 31: 'And the second is like, namely this, Thou shalt love thy neighbor as thyself. There is none other commandment greater than these.'"

Buck closed the Bible. "There are a dozen other passages that echo this. Love thy neighbor. I don't know but one remedy when a community starts acting like this one is, and that's for the decent, God-fearing folks to stand up and be counted. To counsel others to not be spreading gossip, to be more forgiving, to lead the way so we can get this town back to what it ought to be, what it's always been."

Having made his point, he worked the message back around to trying to prick the heart of anybody who might need a large dose of salvation, the standard closing for a sermon. But he knew all of those present tonight, and he felt pretty good about the status of everybody's soul, excepting Doc's. As for Doc, Buck figured he'd need bigger guns than he was firing today to make headway there.

He stood at the back door after the service, alternately passing out handshakes and hugs. Each person assured him that he or she was going to go make a big difference in the community, just as he had asked. He hoped it was true. One thing he'd learned over the years, promises made in the door of the church sometimes didn't even make it to the curb.

◊

The following morning, Raul had a report for Buck as soon as he came in the office. "We had some feedback reported in at shift change."

Buck removed his hat and wiped sweat on his forehead, then

on the hatband. "Shoot."

Raul looked down at the paper, "First, it turns out there were two heavyset gentlemen who spent a night in a room out at the Dixie Lodge about a month ago. They were only there for one night, but they stood out enough for Mrs. Foley to remember them clearly."

"Why?"

"Like you suggested, dark suits, expensive, came in late. At first she was afraid she was about to be held up."

Buck put his hat back on. "What made her think that?"

"She said they looked like gangsters right out of a movie."

Buck shook his head. "I wonder why these guys don't just wear a big sign."

"I bet they don't stick out so bad back where they come from," Raul said. "They probably didn't think about what clothes would help them fit in out here. I'll give them credit, though, they had it worked out by the next morning."

"How do you know that?"

Raul smiled. "They asked Mrs. Foley for directions to a place where they could buy western outfits. They said they were Eastern tourists, and they wanted to get into the swing of things. She sent them to Addison's."

"Did we follow up?"

"Yes, they both bought boots, jeans, straw hats, the works."

Now it was Buck's turn to smile. "Ain't it like a Yankee to think they'll look like a local with brand new duds on?"

Raul nodded. "Yeah, you can see a brand new straw hat about as far as you can see a neon sign."

"I'd say so. I'd also say they tossed Junior's house before they underwent this transformation, because they didn't have boots on out there, at least according to the tracks Little Bear found."

Raul nodded again and looked at his notes. "Yeah, you're right. Let's see, we also had a report from John Redman of a low-flying plane out by his place. He said a month ago would be about right."

"Why didn't he report it?"

"He thought they were only flying pipeline patrol. They do it all of the time out there. When the boys asked him about it, it caused him to think maybe it was a bit late in the day for that."

"I guess that's how planes have been coming and going without attracting attention. Anything else?"

Raul closed his little notebook. "All I got for now. Did you hear about the picket that's walking out at Cox Oil?"

"Picket line? In Clear Creek? You saying they're on strike?"

"Not exactly. The company is going under. Bunch of guys not getting paid. They're pretty hot about it."

"Just what I need." Buck sighed heavily. "Somebody keeping an eye on the situation?"

"Two units."

"I remember when keeping an eye on this little town was a right peaceful job.

Chapter 11

Buck got home to find a young man waiting for him on the porch. He was a nice looking fellow with a solid build and brown hair cut in a full style. He had a very pleasant look to him, yet Buck narrowed his eyes as he said, "Something I can do for you, son?"

"Are you Buck Green?"

"Yes, I am."

He stuck out his hand. "Then you'd be my Uncle Buck. I'm Ruth's son, Wayne Tunnell."

"Wayne? You don't say." Buck put his hand on the young man's shoulder and shook the offered hand. "I haven't seen you since you were knee high to a grasshopper."

"Yes, sir."

"One thing you need to know, son. I'm not much on being called sir.

"Yes, sir."

Buck steered him over to a chair and they took a seat. "So, what are you doing out this way?"

"Mom sent me. You see, I'm having a bit of a difficult time right now, and she said you could help me get things straight in my head, if anybody could. Of course, I know it's an imposition, and if you don't want..."

"Nonsense. I'm right proud she sent you to me. I don't know why she did, or what I can do, but I'm pleased to have you here.

We can kick things around a bit and maybe even help a little. We'll see. Perhaps it's best if we merely spend a little time getting acquainted and not talk about your problems quite yet."

"That's okay with me."

"In fact, I could use a fresh perspective myself. This Jorgenson case I'm working on has me walking in circles. My friend Little Bear said he was ready to get away from the big city for a bit, so we were planning to spend a few days up at the cabin. If there's any place that can help you clear out the cobwebs, that'd be it. He's gotta be the only one around who thinks of Clear Creek as the big city. To everybody else, it's a pretty small town."

"I suppose that would be a matter of perspective."

When the phone rang, Buck excused himself and went inside to answer it.

"Sheriff, this is Penny, there's a riot in progress at the Candlelight Bar."

"Riot? That's a little much, isn't it? Prisons have riots, big cities have riots. We generally have fights, and half-hearted ones at best."

"Nothing half-hearted about this, Sheriff. There's about three dozen hardhats who've chosen up sides and are thumping each other over there."

"First a picket line and now a riot? Why am I not surprised?" He grabbed his hat and breezed by Wayne on the porch. "I've got to go play sheriff for a few minutes. Make yourself at home, and I'll be right back."

Three units were on the scene when he arrived. His officers were failing in their attempts to break it up. Buck pulled the riot gun from a patrol unit, then touched it off three times into the air in quick succession.

The scene stopped like a freeze frame in a movie. Some of the boys actually went to the ground.

"I've had me a bad day, boys," Buck announced over the sudden quiet. "You keep up with this foolishness, and I'm going to dust me some people with buckshot. I'd regret it of course and would probably get into all kind of trouble, but the problem is, I'm in the mood to do it."

Apparently they believed him. Everyone remained still.

"I know what this is all about, and, to be plumb truthful, I can't say I blame you. In fact, what I'd really like to do is take this badge off and get in there and mix it up with you. But being as how I'm getting sorta old and situated somewhat on the small side, that don't seem to make no kind of sense at all."

There was a little grinning and snickering, as the tension noticeably lessened. "Still, I know you got a lot of steam bottled up right now. I guess what I want to do is to let you finish what you started and get it out of your system once and for all. The thing is, the way you're going about this, there ain't nobody having any fun, and somebody might really get hurt."

He turned to Raul. "You still volunteering your time with those kids over at the Boy's Club?"

"Yes, sir."

"Which means you have the gear in your trunk?"

"Some of it."

"Get a couple of head protectors and some gloves." He turned back to the group. "What we're going to do is to go back inside and get comfortable. Any of you who still want to duke it out can jump out there on the dance floor and do it right. I realize some of you aren't going to want to do this without a big group to hide in, but that's okay, too."

Raul leaned over and spoke into his ear. Buck looked at him a moment, then smiled. "Now that's a right interesting idea."

Turning again to the group, he said, "Some of you have been wanting a chance to try the big guy on for years, but you don't want to go to jail for it. Well, the winner of the preliminaries is going to get a shot at the title. He gets to go up against Raul, no penalty attached."

They all filed inside. Buck asked the owner to call Doc at the hospital, then settled into a chair and ordered a Coke. "Now, there's one other little thing." His voice sobered. "We'll be conducting this little dance according to the Marquis of Queensbury rules, which you may be inclined to ignore. To this end, may I point out the referees are duly constituted police officers, and if you don't obey them, they are authorized to pull their nightsticks and turn back into law enforcement personnel. Do I make myself clear?"

Out of breath as he rushed in, Doc plopped into the chair down front they had saved for him. "Glad you called, Buck. I'd have sure hated to miss this."

"I figured it wouldn't hurt to have you here. You're authorized to stop any fight that, in your medical opinion, has gone far enough."

"All right." Doc took a drink. "In my profound medical opinion. Know what started this?"

"It was bound to happen. They didn't get paid and were in a bind. They gotta take it out on somebody and just decided to jump on each other. We might as well let 'em get it out of their system, but I wanted things done so we can keep it under control. Besides, my budget won't stand feeding this many prisoners."

As they waited for the match to begin, Doc leaned over and whispered, "I hate to bring a delicate subject up at such an inopportune time, but what do you think your little congregation is going to think about you hanging out in a bar like this?"

"When they hear the circumstances, I think they'll figure it's okay. If you want, two of my deacons are in here. We can ask them."

Carol served as the referee of the fourth match, to the chagrin of one of the combatants, who protested loudly.

Carol turned to Buck, her face contorted in anger. "Sheriff, I've had it with the bull-headed macho attitude around here. Everybody in town thinks I'm a token officer, just hired because you needed to be able to say you had hired a woman. Nobody really believes I can do my job."

Buck waved his hand in the air. "I don't think people believe that. Not really."

"A lot of them do, a majority of whom are present right at this very time." She glared around, then angled her head at a big fellow nearby. "Sir, I request permission to take this clown on myself and put this foolishness to rest."

"I ain't fighting no girl," the man's lip curled, and his words sounded like a snarl.

"You wouldn't be fighting her, John. She'd be mopping up the floor with you. She's an ex-Marine, hand-to-hand combat instructor with a black belt."

"Don't cut no ice with me." John shrugged.

"Carol, you may be right," Buck slapped his knee. "This may be exactly what you need to establish yourself around here. If he's dumb enough to do this, then you have my permission."

"You mean I get to hit her? When I hit my wife, you arrest me."

"John, you have a green light this time. Personally, I think you're going to have a different outlook on the subject of hitting women when this is all over."

Chapter 12

Buck glanced at the group. The spirited betting had ceased. No one thought Carol had the slightest chance against the big man.

Doc grinned at him, nodding when Buck whispered, "I'll help you cover a bet if you need it."

Buck rocked his chair back on its rear legs. "No bets on this fight? Big macho guys think the little dumpling doesn't have a chance? It's times like this I wish it wasn't against my convictions to gamble. I'd sure be backing Carol's play. I always back my officers, but this time it'd be like shooting fish in a barrel."

Doc's grin sobered. "Well it isn't against my convictions, and I see it exactly the same way. I have no qualms against accepting all the donations you gentlemen care to make. I'm willing to cover all bets." Doc got ceremoniously to his feet, a wad of money in his hand. "I'll take the little lady and offer three to one odds."

"Is the three on him or on her," someone asked.

"It's three to one she will win, of course," he said as if the question were ridiculous "Buck stands behind his officers, and I stand behind Buck. He can't do this, but I certainly can."

"Three to one!" John Sanders exploded. "I got $42 left in my kick. You cover it?"

"Put up your money." Doc said, his grin back in force. "Who do you want to hold the stakes?"

They agreed Buck would hold the money. Bets flowed like

water. The Candlelight Bar was the ultimate bastion of male dominance, and their beliefs were being directly challenged.

While bets were being tallied, Carol stripped her equipment, then pulled off the heavy vest and her uniform shirt, down to her T-shirt. She removed the bulky boots and started doing stretches to limber up.

As she and John faced off, Buck interrupted. "Carol, I'd like this done in a lesson format, if you don't mind."

"You mean with narration and comments, the whole bit?"

Buck gave a single, slow nod. "If you please, just as if you were still instructing the troops."

She stepped back to face the audience. "Men, size is unimportant in martial arts."

The crowd snickered. Someone said, "You gonna think unimportant when John gets hold of you."

She ignored the comment. "It's all about skill, speed, and leverage." She spread her feet to balance her weight, put her hands in a blocking position, then, with her fingers, motioned for John to come to her. "All I'm going to do is defend myself, so the first move is yours."

The big man swaggered as he hitched up his belt, playing to the crowd. "I always heard it was ladies first, but then I guess there ain't no ladies here."

"Whup up on her, John," someone yelled. "The uppity broad needs it."

The crowd yelled and hooted. John circled her, then mimicked her wide set fighting stance as he announced, "Besides, ain't gonna be no first move. Gonna be two hits. I'll hit you, and you'll hit the floor."

"You're all mouth, John. Let's see what you've got."

He took a step toward her and unleashed a huge roundhouse punch intended to put the fight to rest in a single blow, but there was no one there.

She simply ignored the punch as she continued to lecture. "This is the speed option. When the opponent is bigger, it's important to not let him get solid contact, where his superior muscles come into play, or get hold of me, where I lose my mobility."

"We gonna dance, or we gonna fight?" John tossed another swing.

"Your choice, John. So far you haven't shown me a thing."

John waded in, throwing both hands. He still couldn't hit her, and if he got close with a punch, she blocked it aside. Still he advanced, intent on driving her to the wall, where he could get his hands on her.

Unexpectedly, she dropped and pivoted to sweep his legs out from under him. He hit the floor hard with a grunt heard across the room. He was slow in getting up and seemed to be having trouble regaining his breath.

"That was the leverage option. With it, the opponent's size is used against him."

She had been talking to the crowd and was slow turning back to him. He jumped her, grabbing her in a bear hug. The crowd grinned and elbowed each other. They were sure this would be all there was to it. Raul started to get up, but Buck put a hand on his arm to restrain him and smiled. "Don't get in a hurry."

She reached down, put a grip on his hand, painfully separating his hands from her body. Then, suddenly, she spun to take him down to his knees. She took his arm back behind him, obviously causing him great pain. Holding him in a way that appeared effortless, she continued the lecture. "The leverage principle can be applied to individual extremities as well as to the body as a whole."

When she released him, he struggled up, rubbing his arm to restore circulation. Now it was his turn to have slow reflexes. "Don't make the mistake, gentlemen, of thinking a woman is incapable of throwing a solid punch."

John's head came up as her words registered, but he was too late. She hit him with three tremendous, rock-solid blows that snapped his head back with a distinctive pop - pop - pop.

John sat there with a dazed look on his face, shaking his head to clear the cobwebs. Carol continued her lecture, ignoring John's groans. "As soon as John gets his wits about him, he's going to lose his cool completely. This time he will use all his male superiority in a direct frontal attack, no holds barred, which will obviously overwhelm me, a mere female. I think this is the point where we move to the skill portion of the demonstration."

"You got the no-holds-barred stuff right, sister. Right here is where you get yours." John's voice had turned to a growl as he came off the floor to rush her. She intercepted him and gave him a rolling hip lock into the crowd, taking out a dozen men and breaking a table. Carol still hadn't broken a sweat.

He came off the floor again with a noise that was positively primal. She walked in to him, deflecting each blow, each time delivering a subtle, but effective, counter punch. None of her blows missed, and none of his connected. He grabbed for her again to get his breath, and she spun away, driving an elbow to his ear. He dropped like a sack of feed.

"I've enjoyed this exhibition, gentlemen," she said. "It's been a nice workout, and I presume you've learned something."

"This ain't over," John growled as he came up off the floor.

"Yes... it is." Carol jumped into the air, turned with a spinning kick and caught John up beside the head with a foot. The kick was delivered with tremendous momentum knocking him back to roll several times ending up in the corner in a heap. He did not get up.

She didn't even turn to look behind her. Her manner clearly said she intended for the match to be over, and it was. She quietly began to put her gear back on.

The room was totally silent. Some of John's friends went over to get him into a chair. The lights were on in his eyes, but there was nobody home. Carol stood in front of him and waited for him to focus. "Your wife has been in my self-defense class for a couple of weeks now."

She turned to look at the crowd. "Actually, a number of your wives have. My suggestion is to keep your hands to yourself, gentlemen. I've taught them some things much more violent than the moves I've used tonight. They won't possess the skill to keep from hurting someone seriously."

It was clear that everybody was stunned. A man said, "Aww, man, John was the one we were counting on to go up against Raul."

Another guy piped up with, "How about if *she* takes on Raul instead?"

Raul held up both hands, palms out. "Do I look that dumb? Boys, I wouldn't tangle with the little lady with anything less than a bazooka in my hands, but I will take any of you on right now. Heck, I'll take any two, your choice."

There were no takers. The riot was over.

Doc waved at the group. "All right, boys, here's our winnings. You boys know Buck's a part-time preacher and don't hold with gambling, so I'm not gonna stress out his convictions by keeping these winnings. I only did this to prove a point for him. I'm giving it to Harry to pay for the broken table and any other damages."

Buck smiled, nodded. "Thanks, Doc. Now, here's the drill for the rest of the evening. I don't see anybody here fit to drive. You can call a cab or call someone to come after you, or you can continue to drink and turn this little event into a slumber party. Our third shift will take over soon from the officers who are here, and you won't be allowed to leave without sober transportation. You got that?"

As they left, Buck took the owner over to the side. "Now Harry, you know these guys. You know if any of them bet the rent or the grocery money. I'm counting on you to slip it back to them on the sly, you hear?"

"Sure thing, Sheriff."

"You can leave Doc and me out of it, Harry. You can be the good guy."

Harry nodded. Then Buck leaned close and spoke very quietly. "Harry, you know I'll hear if you keep all the money for yourself. It's not a good idea to be on my bad side in your line of work."

Chapter 13

Little Bear had promised to meet Buck at the cabin the following morning. Buck and Wayne left the pickup and horse trailer at the headquarters of the ranch that had leased the cabin site. The owner, another old friend, didn't have any other cabins on his land, which meant there wasn't another cabin within miles of Buck's place.

They transferred their gear from the truck to a pack animal, and in the cold gray light of early morning, rode out for the cabin.

"It's really pretty up here," Wayne said as they rode.

"I get up here as often as I can. It's a place where I can shake off the stress, or maybe work up a sermon."

Wayne looked up at the rustic little cabin as they approached, "That must be it."

"Yup, that's it."

"A porch the full width of the cabin just like at your house. Why am I not surprised?"

"In case you ain't figured it out, I'm big on porch sitting. That rocking chair is a twin to the one I have at home as well. Turn around and look down into the valley behind you and you'll see what I like to sit and look at."

Wayne turned, put his hand on the horse's rump and said, "Oh wow."

The steady climb they had been making on the horses hadn't seemed like much, but looking back the land fell a long ways down to the valley. Fog, or maybe clouds, still hung on a bit in the tree line on either side, and the sun reflecting off the little creek they had just forded sparkled like diamonds.

"That's awesome."

Buck pulled up on the reins and stepped down as they got to the cabin. "First things first," he rubbed his low back as he spoke. "I'll go tend to the horses and you go in and clean the place up a bit. Be sure you wash off the table, that's where we're gonna cook, and maybe eat."

Wayne got down and they unpacked the packhorse and set the provisions on the porch.

Buck turned, "Before you do anything else get this ice and this fresh meat in the ice chest. Can you build a fire in the fireplace?"

"Of course."

"Then do that right after the ice and meat. As soon as I get through out here I'll get us a pot of coffee going and I'll take a piece of that rump roast and put us together a nice stew. That's something we can eat on for a couple of days."

When he came back from tending the stock, Buck nodded approval at the cleanup job. "I'll get started on that stew now, how about you take that bucket and go get some water from the stream. Mind you don't drag the bottom when you dip it up.

When Wayne struggled up the hill with the full bucket, Buck said, "Like I said, coffee is the first order of business. We'll keep that pot on the fire the whole time we're here. We drink a lot more coffee up here in the mountains."

The next hour was sweeping up, wiping dust down, making up beds, and most smelling the aroma of the stew simmering on the fire. Buck added some cornbread in a Dutch Oven and set some coals on the lid to bake it.

It seemed to take forever for it to get done, the rich aroma torturing them, but soon they were headed out to sit on the porch, coffee, stew and cornbread in hand. Wayne pulled up one of the other rockers and they went right to work on the food in a most businesslike fashion. It wasn't until they had each polished off several bowls of the stew that they refilled their coffee cup one more time and leaned back to rock and enjoy the view.

◊

Morning came early in the mountains. The horses began snorting and stomping, making impatient noises to be fed and watered. They woke Wayne up, and he quietly got a cup of coffee so as not to wake Buck up and went out on the porch to watch the sunrise. He was surprised to find Little Bear already there.

Wayne watched quietly as the Indian faced the rising sun and chanted. The Navajo followed the chant by offering a pinch of something from the little sack around his neck to the four directions of the wind. As he finished and headed to the porch, he apparently noticed Wayne for the first time. He responded to the boy's unspoken question by saying, "Ever since *Changing Woman* gave us our rituals, my people have greeted *Dawn Boy* in this manner at the beginning of each new day. I have done it my entire life."

Wayne was interested, "Is it part of your religion?"

"No, my brother, I am a Christian. Buck saw to that, but I still observe the rituals of my people, not as a religious ritual, but to preserve the traditions. I observe them to do honor to my heritage as it has been passed down through the centuries. I do not consider them to have religious significance."

"Who is this changing woman?"

The ladder-back chair creaked as he settled his bulk into it. "Our history has it she is the wife of the sun, the ever-benign soul of mother earth. She gave us all of our ceremonials. It was *Changing Woman* who taught us we must constantly seek *HOZRO*, which is a condition where we are at harmony with our surroundings and at peace with ourselves. When we achieve this, we are said to be *walking in beauty*. All Navajo constantly seek this condition." He smiled. "Even if the stories are mythological, the advice they seek to communicate is sound."

"Oh, I see."

Little Bear nodded in response, then changed the subject. "Buck told me you have had some problems and have come out here to 'find yourself.' Have the two of you had the opportunity to talk?"

Wayne nodded, took a sip of his coffee and answered, "He told me my faith would see me through if I'd trust it. I expected that from a preacher. What I didn't expect was for him to put me to work on the woodpile back at his place and tell me to take this little pad of paper and start making a list. He said life is manageable when we have a list."

"That doesn't surprise me. For him to be at peace with his surroundings there must be logic and order. His lists are his way of getting in harmony with his world."

"That's kinda what he said. He said when we had something

on our mind that we couldn't handle it was generally because we were trying to solve a problem that was too big to get a grip on. He said if we break it down into a lot of small problems that can be addressed, a solution can be found. In other words, make a list."

"Didn't you have a list to do at work?" They looked to see Buck standing in the door. "Maybe a honey do list at home?"

"Sure."

"When you lost your job, did that list go away?"

"Of course." Wayne changed chairs so Buck could have his rocker.

Buck sat down and reached for the coffee pot. "Did it now? Or does somebody else just have it?"

Wayne pursed his lips, "I guess it's somebody else's list now."

"There you go," Buck gestured with one hand, "lists are immortal. There's only one way to finish up a list and when we do somebody else has to add our stuff to their list, along with the chore of getting us planted. Life is just trying to work down our list and keep it manageable."

"That makes sense to me."

Little Bear said, "Buck travels the trail of the head, but I travel the trail of the heart. To me it is important how things feel. The Navajo way is to constantly seek to get in harmony with nature around us."

"The trail of the head and the trail of the heart;" Wayne was struggling to get it, "aren't you two ever on the same trail?"

"Ah, yes," Little Bear nodded gravely, "when the head is satisfied with the logic and the heart is at peace with the feelings, that is the condition my people call HOZRO. That is when we are in harmony with all that surrounds us. It is the condition we seek to maintain."

"That sounds like where I need to be if I can figure out how to get there."

Well, speaking of lists," Buck said, "are you guys going to just listen to those horses complaining out there or is somebody going to go toss 'em some feed.?"

Chapter 14

Monday morning and Buck was not totally ready to start another week after decompressing in the mountains. He entered his office expecting to find a ton of work waiting for him. They had apparently handled everything fine without him. It was good he had competent, well-trained people, but it made him feel a little like he wasn't needed.

Crossing the squad room, Sue stopped him on the way to his office. "These fellows are here for the Rogers brothers," she pointed to two corrections officers.

Buck glanced over the paperwork, before twirling his finger so one would turn around. The fellow looked over his shoulder, then grinned as Buck slapped the paper on his back to sign it.

"Mike still watching them?" Buck asked.

"Yes, sir."

Buck motioned to Raul as he came down the hall. "The Rogers boys are looking at life with no parole. I figure they have nothing to lose and a show of force might be a good idea right now. Keep them from getting any silly ideas."

The prison transfer van was backed in at the end as Mike helped the corrections officers take the Rogers Brothers out. Dark-complexioned and black-haired, Chugg and Zeke Rogers projected an air of insolence that filled the room like a tangible thing. They stood well over six feet and weighed close to 300 pounds each. The rancid, bitter odor that entered the hall with them testified to their contempt for bathing or any form of personal hygiene. Crude jailhouse tattoos shadowed their exposed skin.

"Why don't we stroll out there with them?" Buck stepped through the gate in the short railing. "Wonder why they don't have leg restraints on them?"

"Don't know. They're supposed to."

No sooner had Raul spoken than Chugg swung and put an elbow full in the face of the guard holding his arm. The guard went down hard. The front guard turned at the noise just in time to take a forearm from Chugg .

While Chugg attacked the guards, Zeke took Mike to the wall, choking him with his cuffs. Buck and Raul broke into a run. Chugg leered as he braced for Raul.

That left Buck with the problem of dealing with a guy who carried almost twice his weight and built like a Mack truck.

Zeke turned, dropping Mike to the floor. Several steps ahead of Buck, Raul sacked Chugg like he used to do the quarterbacks in the Southwest conference. Chugg crumbled as Raul's weight drove him into the marble, and his head thumped like a ripe melon as he hit.

Buck followed Raul's lead and plowed into Zeke with everything he had. It felt like he'd run into a wall. All of Buck's breath left him in an audible whoooooooosh as he bounced off and hit the floor. Zeke laughed like a lunatic and reached down to get him. Buck shuddered. He couldn't do a thing. He was toast.

The big fist looked big as a basketball as it drew back for the blow. Buck sent message after message to his muscles, but they didn't respond.

Then, suddenly, Zeke wasn't there. Buck raised himself up on his elbows and tried to clear his head enough to see. Lord, be praised. Carol had come out of nowhere, and tiny as she was, had dropped Zeke like a bad habit. Buck's eyes were wide. The big man had slid completely under a wooden bench.

But he didn't stay down. With a grunt, Zeke came up off the floor and threw the bench aside as if it was an egg crate.

Buck struggled to rise so he could help Carol as the angry convict lunged for her, but his legs wouldn't obey him. He shouldn't have worried, because Zeke wasn't even fully upright when Carol's wicked kick spun at Zeke like a rocket, snapping the convict's head so hard, it appeared it might come off. The big man went down again. This time, he didn't get up.

Buck turned his attention to Raul's battle. Raul was in the process of planting his big fist in the middle of Chugg's face, holding him by a fistful of the front of his shirt. Buck felt like he should call him off, but he knew Raul needed to do it.

"Sheriff?" Carol said.

He waved her off. "See to Mike."

She went over to kneel by the deputy. "I think he's all right. Seems to have just got the wind choked out of him."

He looked around. "How about the guards?"

Raul had moved over to kneel by one of them. "They're coming around. They'll be okay."

Carol helped Buck struggle to his feet. "Get some help in here, and load these varmints up while they're so peaceful."

◊

Buck limped back up to his office. He had enjoyed his time in the mountains, and that little confrontation wasn't exactly how he would have chosen to get back into the swing of things. He rocked back in his desk chair, muscles complaining. He closed his eyes to relax, but instead his mystery came back unbidden to his mind.

He sighed, he couldn't put off working on it any longer.

"Good to have you back, Sheriff," Sue appeared in his door.

"Anything been going on?"

Raul Stuck his head in the door to look around her. "All the things you gave us to check on have been a bust, but there are a couple of interesting developments."

"Well, at least hold off on them until I get a cup of coffee in my hands."

Buck had never been one to have people bring him coffee, but this time when Raul offered, he gratefully accepted. When the big man returned with two steaming cups, Buck took a long sip, eyes closed, savoring the warmth it sent to his body.

Relaxing he eased his feet in their customary place in his middle-side drawer, and said, "Okay, this is probably as prepared as I'm gonna get. Let me have it."

Raul settled into a chair across the desk. "The most interesting thing is, we aren't the only ones hunting Junior."

"No kidding? Who else is looking for him?"

"There are three gorillas out at the Hutton House who have mob written all over them. They've been asking questions all over town. Also, Jack Dulaney reported a break-in out at Junior's ranch. He said it had been vandalized."

Buck froze in mid sip. "Vandalized?"

87

"That's what he said. Looked like a tornado hit it."

"Sounds kinda like a good, professional search job, doesn't it?"

"Yes, sir, it does."

"That doesn't make any sense, Raul. I was pretty much thinking Junior was involved with these folks in some manner. I was even leaning toward the theory of him leaving with them or them doing something with him."

"Yes, sir, I was thinking along those lines as well."

Buck went back to sipping his coffee, weighing the information. Raul waited him out.

Finally he said, "So, why would they be here hunting him *here* if he had already left with them?"

"Makes no sense to me. Gotta be different people for some reason."

"It has to mean we have more players on the field than we knew."

"Do you want me to pick them up for questioning?"

Buck held a hand up in a gesture of resignation. "Questioning about what? We don't have a crime, no body, no nothing. I wouldn't even know what to ask them. Besides, my guess is, these guys have been asked tough questions before by folks who are much better at it than we are. I'll bet they're real good at not answering, too."

"So, what do we do?"

"Let's tag around behind them for a while. Maybe they'll lead us to something."

Raul got up to get started. "A two-unit alternating tail? How about if we use personal vehicles?"

Buck shook his head. "No, I also figure these guys have been tailed by cops before. I don't think we're good enough to do it, being as how we don't ever get to try doing it."

Then he grinned and reached for the phone, "But I'll bet they've never been trailed by a Navaho."

◊

This latest information caused all sorts of excitement when Buck shared it back on the porch. Barney said, "Gangsters, are you sure?"

"We're not completely sure of anything right now, but I've got Little Bear shadowing them. He'll call if he turns up anything."

"So, there's no story in it yet?"

"Yeah, Barney, I think there's going to be a heck of a story, only right now we don't even know what the questions are, much less have any answers. Don't worry, I'll keep you posted."

They sat around for a few minutes, sipping their drinks. Then Doc said, "So, Wayne, how did you like the trip?"

Wayne had just come out of the house, went to the fridge and got a soft drink. "Man, it was great! I feel like a new man."

Doc had his hands folded on his shelf of a belly, loosely holding a cold drink. "So you made some progress getting a handle on your problems?"

Wayne went over to settle in the ladder-back chair. "I didn't make any headway on a single one, but Buck and Little Bear turned me on to some new ways to think about my problems. At least now I'm comfortable with the task of working on them. In fact, I put in several applications for jobs. I kinda like it here, so I thought I might stay for a while."

"That's great," Doc said. "We can always use some fresh blood in the community."

Barney knitted his eyebrows. "Coming from a doctor, that has kind of an ominous sound."

"I suppose, if you took it very literally."

Buck's phone rang. He picked it up to hear Little Bear's voice. "Buck, I got a problem."

"What's up?"

"Those three guys are dragging Jack Dulaney around behind the Candlelight Bar. I think they're fixing to rough him up."

Buck jumped up and ran toward his car. "I'm on the way. Did you put it on the air?"

"Raul and Carol should be here any minute."

◊

No sooner had the Indian put the phone down, than he watched Raul and Carol pull into the alley from both ends, their headlights on the group behind the bar. Raul popped his door open and worked the pump on his shotgun. "I want to see hands in the air, and I want to see them now."

"Don't get excited, Poncho. We're only talking," said the man who seemed to be in charge.

Little Bear smiled as he watched Raul brace the man. He wouldn't blow his cover unless he felt they needed help and he was pretty sure that wouldn't be necessary, not with these two. He looked up as Buck pulled in, lights off, and waved him over.

He put a finger to his lips as Buck ran over to him.

"It doesn't look much like Jack is enjoying your talk, Raul said," Looks to me like he's bleeding and can hardly stand up."

"He's had a little too much to drink, that's all. We were only helping him up."

"Face the wall and keep your hands high. Carol, don't get between me and them, but start at that end and pat them down."

She pulled a .45 automatic from a shoulder holster on the first man, then a dainty little snub nose .38 from a holster on his leg.

"I've got a permit to carry it," the first man growled.

"A Texas permit?"

"A New York permit."

"That's not valid down here, sir." She moved on to the next man, who also had a .45 automatic. He didn't have a second gun, but had a wicked-looking butterfly knife and a pair of brass knuckles in his pocket. "These knuckles have been used. Recently."

"You got a permit for them, too?" Raul asked. "I'll bet the blood is still sticky."

"No, it's too fresh to even be sticky," Carol looked at her finger. She was about to move to the third man when the first one suddenly jerked to grab her from behind. Whatever he had in mind was lost as he flew over her head. He landed hard on his back, but rolled up only to turn right into her famous spinning kick.

"Let's see, where was I?" she said in a matter-of-fact manner. She patted the third man down. "Look at this." She held up a little foreign automatic of some type and a leather sap.

"These guys are rough playmates." She laid the arsenal on the hood, then approached Jack, who supported himself against the car.

"Mr. Dulaney, are you all right?"

"Aw," Jack said, "I guess it wasn't any worse than trying to do eight seconds on a bad old Brahma bull. I need a minute or so to clear my head is all."

They cuffed the trio and put them in Carol's unit. She kept an eye on them while Raul slipped around the corner to meet with Buck and Little Bear.

◊

Buck said, "Little Bear and I were watching ready to jump in if we were needed. But if it wasn't necessary I didn't want them to see him for fear of making it harder to tail them. I don't want to meet them just yet, either. I may have me a little idea or two and I don't want them to know who I am. Take them to the station and let's grill them a little. Little Bear and I will watch through the two-way mirror on the door."

Back at the station, Buck's premonition about them proved to be very accurate. They were very adept at not giving out information. When asked why they were here pushing people around they responded they were bill collectors and sometimes liked to put a scare into people. Threatened with being jailed on assault charges, they seemed content to face them as necessary.

"This isn't getting us anywhere," Buck said. "Jack, do you want to press charges?"

Jack frowned, "Do you want me to?"

"It'd get them off the street and make sure they left you alone for a while. But they'd probably have someone make bail for them by morning. If they're walking around, we may can learn something from them."

He shrugged, "Whatever you think."

"Listen, when these guys come out of the room, I want you to let on that I work out at the ranch with you, which I intend to do for a few days." Buck took off his badge and told his secretary to alert people around the office not to blow his cover.

Raul said, "What are you up to, Sheriff?"

"I don't really know. I'm just playing a hunch."

"No, I'd say what you're doing is looking to get your head thumped."

"I hope not," Buck said. "It's such a pretty head."

Chapter 15

Buck rather enjoyed posing as a ranch hand. He and Jack had worked side by side all day, with Raul in the role of guardian angel, never far away, but usually out of sight. Now, their efforts took them near the mysterious tracks as Buck and Jack strained, trying to put a brace on a damaged leg of a windmill without the thing toppling over on them. Raul trained a pair of binoculars from some mesquite bushes.

It was late afternoon, but still very hot for the type of work they were doing, and their shirts were stuck to their body by the sweat glistening on their chests and backs.

Raul ran over, pointing excitedly. "Sheriff, tell me I don't see what I think I'm seeing."

Buck took the binoculars. A bright light showed in the low western sky, too bright to look at through binoculars. "What in the... "

"It's probably a weather balloon or something." Raul shaded his eyes with his hand.

"Yeah, probably, let's go over a little closer and look." Buck took his gloves off and headed for the truck. "I could use a break."

They drove toward the light for miles. As they approached, it got lower and lower.

"Whatever it is, it's coming down," Raul said.

Then it disappeared. Buck told Raul to head over toward the small hill to their right. "I think the thing came down around here somewhere. Let's get up on this hill and see if we can spot it."

The three men puffed and wheezed their way up the hill. Buck groaned. "I gotta get more exercise, I'm really out of shape. It does surprise me for you to be breathing so heavy, as much as you work out."

Raul leaned to rest his hands on his knees, puffing. "I'm carrying a lot more weight up this hill than you are, Sheriff."

As they topped the rise, they were struck dumb. Sitting below, several miles away, but clearly visible, was an object that looked like a large bright metal dish sitting upside down in the middle of the desert.

The first thing Buck could think of was, he owed Doc an apology. He said as much.

Raul whistled softly. "Me, too, I hope we live long enough to give it to him." Then he keyed his belt radio and called the office. When Penny finally answered, she said, "This place is going nuts, Raul, the phone is ringing off the hook with people calling in UFO sightings. What do you want me to say?"

"Tell them we have people out checking on it. I'll get back to you."

Buck studied the scene, trying to figure out what his next move should be. "The way I see it we got two choices. Resign or go closer and see what we have here."

"Can I have some time to think about it?"

"Well, I don't have to think about it." Jack stared down at the valley, raised his hat to swipe at the sweat they all had dripping down their face. "Seein' as how I don't have to do either one, that's exactly what I plan on doing."

Buck lowered the binoculars. "There seems to be someone moving around outside that thing. It looks like they are doing surveying or something."

Raul held his hand out for the binoculars, adjusted them, then agreed. "Or they could be setting up defenses."

"Why would they be doing that?"

"The thing came down, maybe it's broken."

"Well, you see that mound?" he pointed. "If we came down from that one right over there, we could keep the hill between us and them and get right up close. From the top, we ought to have a pretty good view."

Raul grimaced. "You are still carrying your pistol, right Buck?"

"Why would a working hand carry a gun? Actually, I do have a shotgun in the truck, for snakes and varmints."

Raul gave a long sigh. "One shotgun and a pistol against space phasers or ray guns or whatever they're likely to have? I don't like the odds, Sheriff."

"Well I ain't crazy about it myself, but we ain't going over there to fight anybody. Just wanna see what's going on."

They went back down to the truck, and Jack climbed in with them.

"I thought you weren't going."

"I'm not, but I ain't getting stranded out here on foot a hundred miles from anywhere. I'll stay with the truck, and you boys can go have your look-see."

Buck drove slowly up behind the hill, partly out of dread and partly to keep from raising dust and giving them away. He parked the truck, and he and Raul headed up the slope. A few steps later, Buck turned to Jack. "You want me to leave this shotgun with you?"

"I ain't gonna need a shotgun as long as I got this truck and these legs."

Buck smiled in spite of the lump in his throat and hurried to catch up with Raul. When they reached the top, they slipped over the edge on their bellies, removing their hats.

The thing looked like an upside-down cereal bowl and was made of bright, polished metal. Buck wished he had a camera. Something, people, he guessed, milled around some sort of survey instruments. With all that equipment and the hastily rigged sunshades, it was hard to make out specifics.

Looked like three of them were over near the ship. Buck could see them entirely too well, particularly with the binoculars. They seemed to be of average human height, but they had very large heads and protruding eyes, along with enormous hands and feet.

A scuffling sound behind them brought both Buck and Raul around with weapons ready. Jack appeared, his grin sheepish. "I couldn't stand it, guys. I just had to... great gobs of goose grease! What is that?"

"Got me," Raul said.

Buck just went back to watching. Finally, he turned to his deputy. "Better call it in. Tell Penny to call the Air Force or the Marines or something. Who do you suppose we're supposed to call?"

"I don't know, how about if we start with the Air Force Base over at Abilene?"

"Good idea."

Raul got on the radio and explained what was going on as best he could. He was trying to be professional about it, but his quivering voice was giving him away.

Penny's answered him, and if Raul's voice showed signs of tension, her voice was borderline hysterical.

"What are they doing now?" Buck asked.

Jack passed him back the glasses. "The ones out in the open seem to be working on some kind of computer or something."

Buck focused the binoculars. "That looks kind of familiar." He studied it. "I'll be switched if it ain't an ATM machine."

"It's a what?"

"You know, a bank automatic teller machine."

"Are you telling me these guys came here from Mars or something to steal an ATM? Come on, Buck."

"I'm not telling you anything except some guy with hands the size of a meat platter is standing over there feeding a card into an ATM machine. Whoops, look there, out comes the money. Wait a minute! Those aren't survey instruments, they're cameras."

"Tell me we haven't already called this in."

"Raul, how do you feel about moving to Pakistan?"

"Too close. I'm thinking about the South Pole."

Raul keyed the mike. "Penny, how do we stand on those calls?"

"They've passed me up to some intelligence officer. I'm waiting for him to quit laughing."

"Well, when he gets back on the line, tell him you just learned the deputy who called it in was drunk on duty. Ask him to forget the whole thing."

"I beg your pardon?"

"Do it, girl, and don't say a word to anyone until we get back to explain."

Over the air, they heard Penny say, "You hear that, guys? Raul said not to say anything to anyone until he gets back."

Raul buried his head in his hands. "I wish they *were* Martians so I could go back with them. The South Pole ain't gonna be near far enough away."

They headed down the hill. As they neared the scene of action they heard the director call, "Cut! That's a wrap!"

After introducing themselves, Jack couldn't keep his mouth shut. Pretty soon, the whole film crew collapsed laughing as he relayed the story..

Red-faced, Buck gave Jack a hard look, then tried to bluster his way through, "Why didn't you let us know you were doing this?"

"We would have had everybody and his dog out here watching," the director said. "It would have made it impossible to shoot. We'll go give a story to your newspaper on the way back that should clear up all of those telephone calls."

"So what is it you're shooting?"

"It's a bank commercial using some old science fiction movie props. It's going to be a good one."

"What was the light in the sky?"

"What it usually is, a weather balloon. We set our cameras up so we could photograph only the sun's reflection. We covered the balloon in foil to enhance the effect."

"We must have had the same view. It looked real as the dickens."

"It's certainly the effect we were hoping for."

◊

Buck and Raul braced themselves as they pulled into the courthouse parking lot, it was full of cars with press identification on them. Buck's sighed. Man, this was bad. Jack wouldn't have missed this for the world, but quickly got off to the side.

Raul held out a hand to stop him from getting out of the truck. "I can't believe I'm saying this, but you can't go in there, Sheriff. It would wreck your stakeout at Junior's place."

"I can't let you take the heat on this alone."

"I'm not going to be alone. I'm going to take them to the newspaper office where the crew from the commercial can divert their attention"

A few minutes after Raul entered the office, reporters and camera crews scurried for their cars. Just like Raul had said, they followed the story. Buck waited for several minutes before he eased in the side door.

The media may have been gone, but what he saw stopped him in his tracks. Everyone in the office had wrapped up in aluminum foil.

Mike stepped forward. "Greetings, earthling, take me to your leader." He held up his hand in the familiar four-fingered V made so famous by the Star Trek movies. "Be well."

Buck just hung his head and laughed. There was no escaping it, so he might as well go ahead and take his medicine.

Chapter 16

Buck was preoccupied with the further humiliation he knew waited for him when he got back to his house, a premonition that proved completely valid. He pulled into his drive to find Doc, Barney and Wayne in place on the porch. He got a drink and sat down. It was several minutes before Buck exploded. "All right, all right, drop the other shoe. I can't stand the suspense."

Barney said, "Not us, Buck, there's no challenge. It's no fun when it's so easy. We'll wait for an opportunity that requires a little something on our part."

"Yeah," Doc said, "but you gotta remember that just because these guys weren't the real thing doesn't mean real aliens weren't involved in Junior's disappearance."

"No, but it doesn't mean they were either," Buck said.

Doc nodded. "I'll buy that, as long as you make sure you keep an open mind."

"His mind was pretty open a few hours ago," Barney worked hard keeping a straight face until he lost it and laughed so hard he couldn't get his breath. Doc and Wayne joined him.

Buck could do nothing but sit and shake his head. "I knew you couldn't leave it alone. I just knew it."

Finally Doc recovered enough to ask, "So, nobody showed up out at Junior's?"

Between guffaws Barney managed to say, "Nobody human,

that is?"

Buck ignored the latter. "Not yet. I'll give it a couple more days."

"What are you going to do when someone does show up?" Doc seemed willing to let the teasing go and get serious

"Play it by ear, I guess."

"Are you real sure this is a good idea?" Barney asked.

"Actually I'm not, but I don't have any other ideas."

Raul's car pulled up at the curb. Without a word, he opened the refrigerator and grabbed two beers in one big hand. Since he normally drank only soft drinks, it was a red flag, and, given the fact he had dwarfed the refrigerator while in front of it, everyone heeded the warning.

Buck eyed his deputy. "I owe you a big one."

Raul popped one top. "You certainly do, Sheriff, without a doubt." He turned the can up and drained it without taking it from his lips. The second top hissed when he pulled the tab.

"I'll make it up to you. Sometime, when you need me the most, you're going to look around, and I'll be there."

"Don't give it a second thought, Buck, that account's already paid. You've always been there for me in the past. Speaking of being there, are we going back to Junior's place tomorrow?"

"Yeah, I'll pick you up."

Barney smirked "Well I sure hope you guys don't run into any... "

Raul's head snapped around. His eyes narrowed and his jaw clenched.

"... into any, ah... err... of those gangsters."

Buck intervened, "That's what we're going out there for, Barney. I'd just as soon get it over with."

◊

Early the next morning, Jack and Buck were pitching hay in the barn when the men drove up. Raul was up in the hayloft. Buck signaled him to give the prearranged code of keying his radio to alert the dispatcher to send backup.

They came into the barn, guns in hand, took a wide stance, and one of the hoods said, "Hello, Mr. Dulaney, I believe it is time for us to finish our little discussion."

"I'd just as soon not."

"It is natural for you to feel this way, Mr. Dulaney, but we do not intend the matter come up for a vote. Who is this person with you?" he looked at Buck.

"This here is Buck. He works with me. Thought you met him at the Sheriff's office."

"Perhaps, but we were given to understand you were employed here by yourself."

"I needed help, what with the boss gone. I can't run this place by myself."

"Very well, we shall conduct our business with the two of you. Mr. Black, if you will restrain Mr. Dulaney I will ask him some pertinent questions."

"Very well, Mr. White."

"I don't think that would be a good idea." Buck stepped in front of Jack.

"Please hold on for a moment, Mr. Black. It would appear we

have a volunteer."

Buck held up a hand as if to ward off the implication. "No, I ain't a volunteer, and I can tell you I'm a professional chicken with a low tolerance for pain. I don't see any reason for anybody to get hurt here. Jack and I don't know much, but you are welcome to whatever we know without getting physical about it. It's not like we're at war or anything where we have to keep state secrets."

"We would find this acceptable. We do not mind being persuasive, but it's hot and we really would rather not have to work up a sweat."

"So what is it you want to know," Buck asked.

The corners of the man's mouth turned up slightly, but the result fell short of a smile. "It is very simple. Where is Mr. Jorgenson? This is all the information we require."

Buck tilted his head, "Don't think I wouldn't end this little interview right now if I had that information, but we just plain don't know. The highway patrol found his pickup a couple of months back, and we ain't seen him since."

The pistol the man had trained on them did not waver. "He did not say where he was going?"

"He didn't even say he *was* going."

The man frowned. "You expect me to believe you don't know anything?"

Buck looked down, "No, what I expect is you'll whip up on us some, and, being the wimp I am, I'll start making up stuff to get you to stop since I don't really know anything to tell you. You'll follow up on it and will be madder than a wet hen when none of it turns out to be true. I'd rather not go through all of that, but I will if I have to."

"I would advise you not to lie to us. It does not show the proper respect."

Buck held up his hands, palms out. "Hey, the last thing I want to do is show a lack of respect to a bunch of guys carrying more guns than an infantry brigade, but I know me. If you start laying pain on me, and I don't have anything real to give you, then I'm just naturally going to start making things up to make you stop."

"What was the last thing Jorgenson said to you?"

"We came to work one morning, you see we're only day hands and don't live here. Anyway, Junior wasn't here when we arrived. A couple of days later, the cops told us about finding his truck. What are you guys hunting him for?"

"Mr. Jorgenson has done a disservice to some friends of ours. They feel it calls for some retribution. You might say we specialize in squaring accounts. We are private contractors, and we have a contract to collect this bill that is owed and is now due."

"You saying he owes you money?"

The man laughed. "No, he owes his life, and if you try to protect him, then we're going to throw you in for free."

Buck raised his voice. "I think that's about all we're going to get, don't you think, Raul?"

"Raul?"

There was the sharp but distinctive sound of the slide on a pump shotgun. Raul covered them from up in the hayloft, "What the sheriff means is you've said what we need to hear. Get those hands above your head. You know the pattern on this thing covers all three of you easy at this range."

They dropped their weapons. One said, "Sheriff?"

Deputies burst in from both ends of the barn and began frisking and cuffing the men.

"You mean one of these guys is the sheriff?"

"Sure is," Raul said.

"Which one?"

"Which one do you think?"

"The skinny, hard one. The other is too big a wimp to be a sheriff, by his own admission."

Buck pinned on his badge.

"You? I don't believe it."

"Things ain't always what they seem." Buck looked at Raul. "Did we get it all on tape?"

"Every word."

Buck smiled, but there was no warmth in it. "I'd say you boys are going to be out of circulation for a while."

"You know they'll only send someone else. One way or another Jorgenson is going down."

"We'll see about that."

Chapter 17

"They're right, you know," Doc sipped his drink, "it isn't over. They *will* simply keep sending people until the job is done."

The usual group was assembled.

"I know," Buck said dejectedly, "there has to be something that can be done about it, but hanged if I see a way clear."

Barney said, "So where is Junior?"

Buck ran his hand through his hair. "You know, I'm beginning to have this sneaking suspicion that he's in the witness protection program."

"Really?" Doc's interest intensified. "What makes you think so?"

"Nothing, but little stuff seems to add up that way. For example, it would explain those federal guys I ran into over at Lupe's place, and it might explain those guys in town that everybody thought were gangsters."

"So you think Junior got on the plane he met?" Doc asked.

"Yeah, I'm starting to. And I don't think it was money in the suitcase, I think it was his clothes."

"Very smart, Buck. I always said there weren't no moss growing on you." The voice came from inside Buck's house.

"Junior! What in the world are you doing here?"

The rancher pushed open the screen door. His shoulders slumped under his blue work shirt, and his gray head sagged noticeably. He grabbed a soda.

Barney looked around nervously. "Is this safe? I don't want to get caught in a crossfire."

"Relax, Barney, it's too soon for them to have somebody else after me now that Buck has jailed this latest batch." He raised his drink in salute.

Buck grinned, offering his own glass in salute.

"Everything you said is right on target, Buck. The FBI found out there was a contract out on me and flew in to pick me up. Turns out you spotted both teams who contacted me, though it did take you a while to understand what you were seeing."

"What's this all about, Junior?"

Junior sat on the porch railing. "I witnessed a mob hit and gave testimony on it in Chicago a couple of years ago. It turns out the guy pulling the trigger was Mr. DeGrassi himself. He's a big time mob boss. They don't take kindly to anyone talking out of turn, so they've been trying to cancel my ticket ever since. I came out here and bought my little ranch because I grew up on one. The FBI set me up on it. I can't say I like having to give it up."

"So why are you back?"

"We were up in Portland, Oregon, when I started seeing signs we were being shadowed. You learn to notice such stuff when people are after you all the time. You know what I mean?" I just got to thinking that I trust you more than I trust the ones they have assigned to me."

"Very flattering, Junior, but I don't know a thing about running a protection operation." Buck sat there and thought a minute, then he made up his mind. "So, if I'm not qualified to play their game, then why don't I make them play mine?"

"I don't understand," Junior admitted.

Buck tossed his drink can into the container at his feet. "Anybody they're likely to send will have to be a creature of the city. It's their environment. The size of our town would be an impediment to them, granted, but they would eventually figure out how to get around it."

"So what do you have in mind?"

Buck got up and walked over to Junior. "I have in mind taking them out to my world. We're gonna go hole up in my cabin. Let's see how these big city boys do with nature, not to mention a big Indian, on our side."

Little Bear smiled, "This is to my liking. My people have not been on the warpath for many moons." Dropping the movie dialect he added, "Actually, I 've never tried it myself, but always wanted to."

"That's not a bad idea," Junior nodded.

Wayne said, "Can I go, Buck? I still don't have a job, and I sure love it up there."

Buck turned to face him. "I don't think so, Wayne. This is likely to be dangerous, and no place for amateurs."

"Maybe you could use a city boy's viewpoint to help you figure out what this guy is likely to do."

"Well, maybe, but Ruth would never forgive me if I got her boy shot."

Wayne lowered his head and looked up at him in a sly look. "If I got shot, wouldn't it mean you got shot, too?"

"Probably."

"So you wouldn't have to worry about facing mom at all."

Buck smiled, and Wayne knew he was going back to the mountains.

◊

On the way to the cabin this time, Buck stopped at the forest service station. A cellular phone wouldn't work that far out, and his radio signal couldn't make the distance from cabin to town, but if he rigged an antenna, he could reach the ranger station and could arrange a patch through to Clear Creek. The ranger, Bob Jennings, was more than happy to cooperate.

Little Bear already knew what he was going to do. "You guys go get settled in, but I'm going to be spending my time out in the open away from the cabin."

"Why?" It was clear Wayne didn't understand.

"I need to be out away from the cabin where my ears can be in tune with the sounds of the woods."

Wayne said, "That sounds like fun, can I join you?"

Little Bear was trying to walk the line between hurting the young man's feelings and being able to do what he needed to do. "I do not mean to be rude, little brother, but it would defeat my purpose. The sounds you would make sleeping, even turning over or shifting in your bedroll, would mask the noises I need to hear."

When they got close to the cabin, Little Bear branched off to find a campsite that would provide a good view of the whole valley, as well as of the cabin and its approaches. The rest of the party went in to set up housekeeping and brew a pot of coffee.

◊

Finally alone, Little Bear spent several hours scouting the area, seeing what wildlife was there, refreshing himself on his knowledge of the trails, making himself at home in the woods again.

He and Buck spent a lot of time up here, but for this task, he needed more than casual knowledge of the area. He also needed to get in touch with his warrior heritage.

He needed to begin to think like a hunter.

Chapter 18

Antonio Torelli's first objective, as he drove around town in his rental car was to see how he had to dress and how he had to act in order to not stand out among these people. Tony was not only a professional hit man, he was a chameleon. He was average build, average height, no distinguishing marks and never did anything to call attention to himself.

A majority of his success was because he could fit in anywhere. He accomplished that by studying the locals then acquiring a wardrobe to appear to be one of them. After a couple of hours, he used a usual trick to secure his wardrobe.

Tony sat reading a newspaper on a bench outside of a Laundromat until a man the appropriate size came along. He watched as the man washed his clothes and put them into the dryer, then he went over to stick his knife into the tread of one of the man's tires.

When a lady came by he casually said, "What a shame, looks like someone has a flat tire."

"Oh, my," she said. "Perhaps it's someone inside? Do you think?"

When he merely shrugged, she seemed to make up her mind and headed forcefully to the door of the Laundromat.

He heard her say, "Does anyone belong to the old green pickup out here?"

Sure enough, the owner came out with a curse on his lips, but he got busy changing that tire. As he plied a wrench on the lug nuts, Tony went inside in, picked up the already broken-in wardrobe, and left by the side door.

Step two would involve getting something to eat and maybe picking up some information about Jorgenson in the process. He would also steal a well broken in cowboy hat on the way out of the restaurant.

After eating and acquiring his headgear he returned to his hotel, prudently located in the neighboring town 35 miles away. There he settled in to relax for the evening. Tomorrow he would hang out in a couple of the bars back over in Clear Creek. Only after he had been there a while would he pass a chance remark about having an old army buddy he thought lived here in Clear Creek, which ought to be sufficient cover for gathering information.

He opened one of the cold beers he had iced down in his waste can and settled in to watch an old western movie on television. *I was born in the wrong century*, he thought as he watched. *I would have been a gunfighter if I had lived back then. I guess it's exactly what I am now, only I have to hide it in these times. Back in those days I would have been as big a superstar as a pro quarterback.*

◊

Little Bear showed up at the cabin, timing it perfectly as Buck had gotten the fire going outside with the steaks on the grill. "How did you know?" Buck asked.

"Are you kidding me?" The big Indian almost smiled. "I could smell those steaks sizzle clear down the mountain." He licked a finger and held it up. "It's downwind."

Buck got up to turn the steaks. "Won't be long now."

While they were eating, Little Bear asked Buck when he thought the man would come.

"Wouldn't surprise me for him to be in town now, but I figure it'll take him a couple of days to work out where we've gone." Buck cut off another big bite and poised with it speared on his fork. "This cabin is no big secret. He'll come eventually, but it'll probably be two or three days. I've got the forest rangers and the ranch hands down below looking for a car sitting around with nobody in sight. I figure we'll get ample warning."

Little Bear said, "Good, I've been getting my warriors ready."

Buck finished chewing the bite, swallowed, and said, "Warriors?"

"Yes, I have been trapping some animals I intend to use on him and have spotted some more."

"What are you going to use them for?"

"Not much, simply to harass him and keep him from getting sleep. I don't want him thinking straight. I have been setting up some simple human traps, too."

"Traps? What are you going to do with him if you catch him?"

It was Little Bear's turn to pause and swallow. "They aren't intended actually to snare him, but to stick and scratch him, make him uncomfortable They're made so naturally I doubt if he will even see they were made by human hands."

"You doing this mostly to tire him out?"

"Yes, and to frustrate him. I want him to clearly know he is out of his element. I think this whole thing can be pulled off without anyone getting hurt."

Wayne said, "I'd sure like to be in on some of it."

"Yes, little brother, I would welcome the company. Also, as I intend to work shifts on him, I can use you to watch him during the day so I can get some sleep. I mean to spend most of the night aggravating him."

"Chief," Buck said, "this guy is going to be dangerous, a real killer. You're talking about this as if it were some sort of game."

"I know very well how dangerous this man can be. Trust me, I will not underestimate him, nor will I allow your young cub to be in any danger. In spite of this, however, I do think this is going to be most entertaining."

◊

Tony could be a convincing drunk. After he had soaked up a few, he bought a round for some local ranch hands. He got to talking with them, but they weren't giving up much information.

His plan had unfolded flawlessly to this point, with one minor exception. It hadn't occurred to him someone would recognize the hat. Back home, a hat was a hat was a hat. Apparently out here, a hat takes on a its own character. He found this out seconds before he was about to leave when a voice at his elbow said, "So you're the turkey who stole my hat."

"Your hat? This is mine."

"You're a liar." The cowboy pointed, "that there's the way I crease my brim. I recognize the sweat stains, and up there is the gouge an old one horned steer made in it when I tried to get him out of a mud hole."

"You don't say?" Tony removed the hat and looked at it. "Maybe it is yours, I didn't look very closely at it. It somewhat favors mine."

"The only thing worse than somebody who'd steal your hat is somebody who would lie about it after he done it." Big Tom Kimble didn't mince words, and he only knew one way to go: straight ahead. The scars on his face were testimony to his predisposition to settle things the way they should be settled, man to man.

Tony had been around the block enough times to know when a fight was unavoidable. The slum he grew up in was ample training grounds. He said, "But how do you account for my name being in the hat?"

"What?" The cowboy looked into the hat as Tony held it out. As he looked inside, Tony jammed the hat onto the cowboy's face and hit the man in the face hard, three times in quick succession. It should have been enough... but it wasn't.

Falling back against the wall, the cowboy managed to pull the hat off his face and give a crooked grin.

"Well, now, I didn't really think you'd be up for the dance. I figured I'd just whomp you a little, and that'd be it." The man clearly relished the opportunity. The man spit on his hands.

Oh, come on. Tony rolled his eyes. Spitting in your hands?

The man waved his arm. "Gimme some fighting room." People moved back to comply

The man waded in and threw a huge punch, which Tony ducked under. Tony let go with a big one of his own. It landed right in the man's solar plexus and should have taken his wind, particularly if he had been drinking. It didn't do nearly as much as Tony expected.

The man staggered back a few steps. "Will you give me some fighting room?"

He came back in a rush, trying to lock Tony in his grip at close range. Tony side-slipped and threw the man over his hip. The cowboy rolled and rather than sprawling on the floor, landed on one knee. Tony followed up by kicking him in the face, but the man saw it coming and it deflected off the side of his head. It only seemed to make the man madder and, he surprised Tony by being quick enough to grab his heel and push it on up, throwing Tony flat on his back.

The cowboy was on Tony like a cat, pinning him to the floor by holding the front of his shirt with his left hand while he popped him with a half dozen hard right hands. Tony's lights went out.

When Tony came to, he was still lying in the floor. Several cowboys stood at the bar or sat at nearby tables. Someone said, "Your boy is coming around."

The cowboy looked down at him. Tony tried to rally his senses for another round, but instead the man grinned and said, "I guess we figured out whose hat this is, didn't we?"

At Tony's nod, the man held out a big hand to help him up. "You put up a pretty good scrap. I enjoyed it. Come on over, and I'll buy you a drink." The man offered him an old hat. "Here, you can use this one until you find out what really happened to yours. Drunk or sober, next time you had better make sure which one you're picking up. Once we get one trained to our head, we don't

117

much like to give it up."

Tony smiled weakly. The beer stung the cuts in his mouth, but it tasted good. Now that he'd proved himself, folk seemed to open up, telling him Jorgenson, a local rancher, had gone to the mountains on a trip with the sheriff. He even managed to find out the approximate location of the sheriff's cabin.

He left the bar with unfaltering steps that didn't match the alcoholic stupor he'd pretended. Instead of going back to his motel, he drove all the way to Midland to an army surplus store to get the camping equipment he needed to go after his quarry. He didn't know how long it would take, so he got a sleeping bag, canteen, ax and a bunch of freeze-dried meals that only needed water added.

Tony was actually looking forward to this. He had always wanted to try camping. He would have the opportunity to do it and take care of his business at the same time.

Back at his room, he unpacked the rifle and scope from its aluminum case. He put it together and cleaned it, then put the carrying strap on it. It would be easier to carry with a strap than it would be to lug a case. Besides, this would keep it closer to hand.

Early the next morning, he headed up into the mountains. He checked his directions at a little store, then drove up the canyon that led to the ranch. He parked his car off the road down by the stream and began his adventure.

◊

The forest ranger called Buck on the radio. "We found a parked vehicle this morning. Can't be sure, but I think your guy is on the way," the ranger said. "And your office called to say someone was asking around about Junior, but they could get no information on him and not even much of a description. Seems the man managed to get crossways with Tom Kimble and had picked up a few lumps for his trouble." The ranger laughed. "They said the guy held up his end pretty well."

Buck put down the microphone. "He sounds like a pro, going up against Tom like that."

Little Bear agreed. "Where did they say his car was?"

"On the stream down below the ranch headquarters. Beyond that, few people know exactly where this place is, so he'll have to ask at the ranch. They won't tell or will mislead him, but at least we'll know for sure that it's our guy."

Little Bear stood and drained the last of the coffee from his cup. "Very well, my friend. It's best we establish contact so we will know where he is at all times." He looked at Wayne. "Come, my young friend. Your education begins."

Buck eyed the Indian. "I'm holding you to your word. Don't you go letting him get hurt."

"Have no fear, we will not get close to our quarry. We merely wish to find his trail and keep tabs on him."

"Okay, if you say so." Buck retrieved a box with three radios in it. "These radios won't reach back to my department, but we can keep in touch with each other even up here, unless you get behind a tall hill."

Little Bear nodded, took two of the radios, picked up his rifle and headed out.

Wayne pointed at the gun. "Don't I get one of those?"

"I'm sorry, but if you had one you might be tempted to use it.

I would much rather you be thinking in terms of hiding than in terms of fighting." Little Bear looked at Buck. "He's your cub. Do you agree?"

"I do." To Wayne he said, "I think the chief is right, at least for the time being. When it gets down to the lick-log, things may change, but for the now..."

"Hey, no problem. I was only asking."

Buck sighed as the two of them disappeared down the valley. He couldn't help but worry.

Chapter 19

Wayne and Little Bear walked in silence for some time before the big Indian said, "Little brother, earlier we spoke of the condition of *HOZRO,* which is a way of life for the Navajo?"

"Yes, and I've been giving it a lot of thought."

"In a large city I think it would be a condition of the mind and would require a lot of inner searching to achieve it. Out here in the woods, it can be very real. We can become part of the countryside around us, and it a part of us. I think if you can get a feeling for it here, where it is close and personal, then you have a greater chance back in the city."

Wayne looked intently at him, "How do you become part of the woods?"

"First, you must accept that it is not your enemy. True, it can be demanding, as you would understand if you were out here in a raging storm with no protection. Yet even then the forest is your friend, if you will look to her for help."

"But we do have an enemy out here."

"Yes, we do, and we will soon find him. Then we will use our friendship with nature to his great disadvantage. If he were a mountain man, then it would be us against him and would be more difficult. Since we know he came from the city, it gives us many advantages."

"Like what?" Wayne's voice was a little breathless from the

uphill climb.

"All in good time. Our immediate objective is to keep him misdirected, to tire and frustrate him so that he cannot think clearly." He put a hand on Wayne's shoulder. "But first, we must find him."

◊

Tony's feet hurt, which made him mad. He muttered to himself, "Much as I paid for these fancy hiking boots, they shouldn't be killing me like this. "When I get through icing this dude, I think I'll go back and stick up the place I got 'em from before I leave. It'd teach them to take advantage of a guy simply because he's from out of town."

Tony grinned at the prospect, then suddenly said, "What am I punishing myself for? It isn't like I'm in any hurry. Besides, I'm hungry."

He found a shady spot, and as he crouched down he fell back, overbalanced by the heavy pack. For several minutes, he lay helpless, trapped on his back like a turtle, unable to escape its grasp. Finally, he wiggled out of the pack and got up.

He looked down at the offending pack, trying to figure out a better way of doing things so he wouldn't get into such trouble anywhere near his quarry.

He used his little ax to cut down a small tree to build a fire. He'd brought along a can of charcoal starter fluid. It worked on his barbecue. Ought to work as well here.

It didn't. He worked at it for over an hour before he began to keep any kind of flame on the wood. It didn't catch until he used small twigs and grass.

He swore to himself as he unpacked his little cooking set and headed to the stream to get some water. *Why did I build that fire so far from the stream?*

He reread the directions on his pack of food while the water boiled. When it was ready, he sat back to eat. "Whew!" he made a sour face. "This sure isn't Mama Luigi's. But it's hot, and it fills me up."

He reached into his pack, pulled out a bottle of wine and a collapsing cup. He took a sip, held it on his tongue, then gently sat back and relaxed. He smiled as he rolled the cup between his hands and looked out across the valley. For the first time all day, his new camping avocation brought a pleased sigh. "Okay Jorgenson, now where in the world are you?"

◊

Little Bear stopped to point to the plume of smoke. "There is our rabbit, little brother."

"How do you know it's him?" Wayne asked.

"Who else would be out here except for ranch hands, our rabbit, and ourselves? The ranch hands would certainly not build a fire out of green wood. In fact, there is little reason for them to build a fire at all. They eat, and eat well, back at their headquarters."

"So, what do we do?"

"We circle around this way so that we may look down on him and take his measure."

They came up the backside of the ridge. Little Bear didn't

want the man to hear any noise Wayne might make as he climbed. He himself would make barely any noise at all.

As they climbed, Little Bear asked Wayne what he heard. After a little prompting, Wayne began to see the only noises were those he made. Little Bear began to show him how to place his feet to avoid rocks that might slide or twigs that might snap. "Your foot comes down hard on your heel, while the Indian walks toe first. If there is something there, even in the darkness, we feel it and make the adjustment in our step."

Wayne was obviously trying, but Little Bear knew it would not do to let him within earshot of the man, even if the man was a tenderfoot.

On top of the ridge, Little Bear slipped out of his small pack, took his hat off, and slid up to look down at the man through a bush. Wayne followed his lead.

"There is our quarry, look at that fire. If he had a wet blanket he could send smoke signals with it, and look how far from the stream he made camp." Little Bear shook his head. "You see how he has camped up against the base of the hill? If it rains, he will awake to find his bedroll full of mud. I was right. The man is a complete stranger to the ways of the woods. Even so, this is not his night camp, or if it is, he will have to move again before daylight."

"Why?"

"The grade he has chosen is very comfortable for sitting, but it is too steep for a bedroll. If he tries to sleep in this way, he will have to move down to level ground long before morning. Not only that, but he only picked up enough wood to make his cooking fire, and he's letting what he has burn down. By the time he decides he needs to build the fire back up, it will be too late, and he'll have to completely start over again. My guess is, when he finally figures it out, he will move closer to the water as well."

As they watched, the man fell asleep. They made themselves a cold meal of summer sausage, cheese, and crackers washed down with a thermos of coffee. Soon, the shadows began to lengthen, and the man turned his attention to trying to coax his fire back to life. After several futile attempts, the man gathered his gear to move closer to the stream.

As the man set down his pack Little Bear allowed himself an enormous smile. "I hoped he would do that."

"Do what?"

"Like the pendulum he has swung too far the other way. I thought he might. He was too far from water, but now he has chosen to make his camp on the sand bar by the stream. If it rains, he will be within the stream bed."

Wayne looked around. "I don't think there's any great chance of rain."

"We shall see, my young friend, we shall see."

The Navajo slid down from the top of the ridge and stood up. "I think Buck must have something excellent to eat by now. Our friend will be occupied for quite some time making his fire out of green wood again, so let us go see."

They smelled the roast Buck had cooked before they got to the cabin door. Little Bear leaned over the pot. Buck had used a can of mushroom soup and added potatoes and onions. Little Bear and Wayne joined the other two at the table.

Buck swallowed, setting down his fork. "You find our boy?"

"He is where I thought he would be," Little Bear said.

"So now what?"

"I will keep an eye on him tonight and provide him some entertainment. I will take Wayne back with me after I come in for breakfast tomorrow."

"Entertainment?"

"You know the beaver dam down here? Where the little swimming pond is?"

"Yes."

"If I breach it, it will send a wall of water down on our friend. It will wash a major part of his stuff away as well as soaking him and all of his gear. It will take him most of tomorrow to get his stuff together and get all of it dry. By that time, I will have more interesting things planned for him."

Wayne raised his brows. "It's a shame to mess up the pond, though."

"This will only lower its level. The beaver will have the damage repaired before the night is over. Then, after the first rain, it will be good as new."

"I'd have never thought of that," Buck said.

"I told you the animals would be my warriors."

◊

Tony laid in a supply of wood. He had even figured out it needed to be wood that had lain around long enough to be dry. He built the fire up to where it burned brightly and snuggled into his bedroll. He yawned, exhausted.

The water came through like a freight train, sweeping

everything before it. One minute Tony was asleep, the next he was choking, swallowing water. Then, as quickly as it came, the surge was gone, and he was left sputtering and choking in the middle of the stream.

He crawled out of the soaked bag. The stream now ran gently down its original course. The water had extinguished his fire and washed away his equipment. He felt chilled to the bone.

It took a long time to gather enough dry grass, leaves and twigs. Without a flashlight, he seemed to be hunting by Braille.

Eventually, he got a little fire going on a high spot well away from the stream. He nursed that fire all night, trying to get some warmth back into his body.

◊

Little Bear slept peacefully up on the ridge. He awoke briefly when he heard the man rummaging for firewood, but once he had assured himself the man was not coming his way, he fell back to sleep.

With the dawn, the man built the fire up as large as he could, then went off in search of his gear. Several hundred yards downstream, he found his pack and everything in it intact, though soaking wet.

Little Bear watched him hang things out to dry. Satisfied this would take quite a while, he went back to the cabin to get his breakfast.

Chapter 20

They had a long, leisurely breakfast, after which Little Bear took Wayne back with him to find their man. Again they came up behind the man on the ridge.

The man was fixing something to eat, clothed only in his shorts. Every so often, he checked his clothing. The disappointed expression revealed his lack of success.

"Wayne, you are a creature of the city, put yourself in his place. You are down by that fire, you don't know where the person you seek may be found. Where would you look first?"

He handed Wayne the binoculars and cautioned him to look only from the shade and through the protection of the little bush. He wanted no movement seen, nor any reflection to come off the lenses of the glasses.

After a close inspection Wayne said, "I think I'd follow the trail by the stream. It's not much of a trail, but it's all I see."

"I think our friend will come to the same conclusion. While the trail does not lead to the cabin, if he continues to follow the stream long enough, it would lead him there."

"So how do we prevent that from happening?"

"Come, I will show you."

They went to intersect the stream and the faint path out of sight of the camp. Before they got too close to it, Little Bear used a small folding shovel from his pack to dig up a relatively tall, very fat bush, which he planted in the middle of the trail.

"Is that thing going to live?" Wayne asked.

"Probably not, but it won't change in its appearance for several days."

The Indian followed the stream and returned with a couple of good-sized logs. Tying a rope to them to make a drag, he created another path from the original one, across the stream, and out on the other side. He told Wayne to sweep behind the drag with branches to erase any harsh marks.

"This wouldn't fool anyone used to the ways of the country in the least, but I think it may be enough for our city boy."

They used the drag back over the hill in a wide circle to a place that allowed them to keep watch from the other side of the stream.

Wayne seemed puzzled. "We're back at his camp."

"Yes. When he leaves, we will drag the new path to join the old one, making a big circle. If he does not pay close attention, he may loop around several times before he notices."

While the man napped, they made three passes with their drag across the new trail. Then they settled in to have another cold lunch.

The mana awoke a bit later and prepared his own meal. He had almost finished when an afternoon shower began. He cursed loudly as he ran to grab his almost-dry clothes. He was too late.

The Indian's big belly shook in silent laughter. "He's in this camp for another night now. Let's go see what Buck has on the stove."

◊

At dusk, Little Bear returned to the ridge, carrying a sack with two good-sized rattlesnakes, a non-poisonous grass snake, and a couple of big sets of rattles from snakes that had gone on to the big snake pit in the sky. Little Bear put one of the big rattlers in the spot the man used to relieve himself.

Little Bear noticed how diffident the man seemed as he approached his makeshift toilet seat. It wasn't quite dark when he sat down on the log, which served instead of a dug latrine

Little Bear had already noticed the man's toilet paper was ruined by the flood and he was having to make to with leaves from plants, but it was very unsatisfactory. He was about to find it even more so, as Little Bear had been removing suitable plants from the area of the log and using two fairly long flat sticks, had placed several plants with curious clusters of three leaves within reach. Any boy scout would immediately know them as poison ivy, however, at the present time the man would find there were no boy scouts available to warn him.

Little Bear waited for Tony to complete his project and laughed to himself as the man used the plants provided for the cleanup work. As the man stood to fasten himself back up, the Indian used another long forked stick to drop the big snake down behind him. The very angry snake immediately coiled and loudly announced his intention to take his frustration out on someone.

There were no targets available, though, as the man high-stepped through the brush like a running back dancing across the goal line.

His eyes were wide as saucers as he looked back at the woods, and his hands shook as he added instant coffee to a cup of hot water. Little Bear shook his head and muttered, "Tenderfoot," with contempt as he poured himself a cup of real coffee from his thermos.

After the man got to sleep, Little Bear slipped closer and tickled the man's face and neck with a long willow branch. That woke him. He slapped, scratched and cursed.

Act two was not long in coming. Little Bear had been waiting for the oil from the plants to begin to burn the man's hands and rear end. And because he'd touched his face and neck, the itching started up there, too. He jumped up and took a bar of soap with him to the stream.

While he was at the stream, Little Bear slipped into the camp and put the small grass snake in the nice warmth of the man's bedroll, so it was waiting for the man when he climbed back in to try to sleep. The itching made him squirm, and pretty soon the snake showed himself.

The man tore the zipper from one entire side of the bedroll trying to get away from the snake. Little Bear could see his hands tremble as the man huddled over his fire, muttering, "Snakes... snakes... snakes everywhere."

Up on the ridge, Little Bear slept well, awakened periodically as the man collected firewood, beating the brush ahead of him with a long stick and swearing incessantly as he scratched.

Chapter 21

Little Bear didn't go back to the cabin for breakfast as he knew the man's misery would cause him to get an early start. When he didn't show, Wayne came to look for him and met him coming down backside of the ridge.

"We missed you at breakfast. Are you leaving?"

"Changing positions. Our rabbit is on the move. I'm going to get close to the hidden trail in case he does not take the bait. I need for you to go to the end of the false trail. After he gets out of sight, extend the trail with the drag on down to the stream and cause it to join up with the trail behind him, then hide the drag by pulling it upstream in the water until it can sit on the bank somewhere out of sight. Can you do that?"

Wayne smiled, "No problem."

"Hurry then. He will be coming soon."

"What are you going to do if he follows the wrong trail?"

"I am putting our friend, the rattler, out along the trail where he will be easily seen. I want this man to have snakes on his mind, if he doesn't already."

"Okay. I'm off," said Wayne.

◊

Tony gathered his gear and started down the trail. He itched so badly, all he could think was that he needed this contract over and done with so he could get to a doctor. This was killing him.

Not a hundred yards down the path, he heard an angry, whirring sound, like an insane baby with a rattle. He froze, searching for its source. There it was, back off the trail, coiled and deadly. He had no idea how fast rattlers could move, but as long as it was out of reach and coiled, he figured he could sneak past.

He'd have liked to shoot it, but the sound would carry too far. No sense warning his prey.

Tony muttered to himself. "Can't believe people actually come to this damnable, biting, scratching, snake-ridden place. Must be masochists." He kicked at a stone. "You can have my share of camping out."

He came to the fork in the trail and followed it.

◊

Shortly after the man disappeared on the trail on the other side, Wayne returned to Little Bear's side.

"You get it done, little brother?"

Wayne was out of breath as he dropped to the ground. "Probably not as well as your trail, but I think it'll do."

"I'm sure it will. Our friend is badly distracted this morning, so I doubt he is very observant. Tell me, my friend, did you possibly bring some fresh coffee with you?"

Wayne produced a thermos from his pack. "Buck said you'd be needing some."

Little Bear quickly pulled a cup from his own pack. "A wise man, our sheriff."

Little Bear brought Wayne up to speed on the night's happenings as they sipped the coffee.

133

Wayne laughed. "One thing you can say for this guy, he's nothing if not determined. I would have gone home long before this"

"Our friend is obviously quite the professional, and very dedicated to completing his mission. Well, he will be coming back around on the circle before long, so you need to go over there on the other side of the creek and find some heavy brush to get in." He produced a big set of snake rattles. "If our rabbit tries to go up your side of the stream, shake these vigorously. If he tries to maneuver around you, be very still and make sure you aren't seen. I will entertain him in a similar manner if he tries to go past our false end of the trail."

◊

Downstream, Tony trudged along the path, hoping he'd get somewhere soon. Before he knew it, another of those blasted rattlers crawled into view Terrified, he stiffened until it was safely past, then, watching it, he continued on.

On the next lap the snake was not there, but the man was still unaware he was going in circles. He was too busy scratching, cursing, and following the path. This time, however, as he got to the false fork and started across the stream, he saw a granola wrapper he had thrown down.

The man leaned over the wrapper. Little Bear heard his puzzled words. "These are all fresh tracks," and saw him set his foot down beside the tracks. He then said, "They're *my* tracks! I'm going in circles. What kind of crazy trail goes around in circles?"

The man returned to the path and tried to go around the bush

Little Bear had planted. "Damn snakes, they're everywhere." He stared at the bush. "Can't see a blamed thing. I'd better not get any closer."

He crossed the stream and started to go up the other side toward Wayne's hiding place, as Little Bear had predicted. Again he was met by the nasty whirring sound. Here he didn't even pause, but hurried down the trail, looking for another turnoff.

It took the better part of an hour for him to make a circle of the trail, which meant he had been walking for hours. He came again to the stream and crossed it. This time, he noticed there was a fork in the trail, so he took the left hand fork. It was only a matter of minutes before he walked back into his campsite again.

"What the..." He threw up his hands.

◊

They watched as he stood there for a minute, confusion clear on his face. His shoulders rose and fell with a deep sigh, then he slumped down to unpack his cooking gear and began to make a fire.

Little Bear said, "Let us go eat, too. Our friend is tired and will rest now."

"I could eat."

"It is a shame, little brother. If I had seen him drop that wrapper and retrieved it there is no telling how long we could have run him around that circle."

Wayne laughed, "I think you're right."

◊

Tony ate his freeze-dried stew mechanically by the small fire. He was exhausted, and the itching would not let up. Should he go find help and come back to do the job later? He didn't like that one bit, quitting on a job wasn't his style. Antonio Torelli's never failed to execute a contract.

That brought a smile. Execute was certainly the operational word.

Trouble was, he was too miserable to appreciate his joke for long. He gathered up his gear, saying, "I have to take another try at it."

Like a robot, he started back down the trail, but when he got to the fork where the trail circled back in, he stopped and looked at the way he had been going. This time, he took the other fork, heading the opposite way.

When he got to the top of the rise, he stopped and ran his fingers through his hair. He looked around, not wanting to retrace his steps, so he decided to take a try going across the valley. Re-adjusting the weight of the pack on his shoulders, he started walking, zombie-like, thinking only of putting one foot in front of the other as he walked.

Suddenly reason returned. A short way in front of him was a windmill with a man working at its base.

The ranch hand looked up as he approached and said, "Howdy, you lost?" He pulled off his gloves and started to shake hands before he noticed Tony's condition. "Holy cow! Looks like you got into some poison ivy. Hope you don't mind if I don't shake hands."

"No, I quite understand. I wouldn't touch my hands either,

except they're attached to me. In answer to your question, I don't know if I'm lost, but I don't seem to be able to match up the directions my friend gave me to his cabin with my present surroundings."

"Your friend?"

"Yes, Buck Green, you know him?"

The old man sat on the edge of the water tank. "Reckon everybody knows Buck."

"You know his cabin?"

"Haven't ever been there," he pointed with the hammer he was holding, "but I think it's about six or seven miles over that-a-way."

"I'm very obliged to you," Tony meant it sincerely. "I don't suppose you have anything for this itch."

The man got up, holding up a hand with the index finger raised. "I've got a little calamine lotion. It'll help as much as anything. Mostly, though, it just has to wear off."

Tony followed him over to his horse. "What would a doctor give me?"

"Same thing, probably. They try to subdue the itch a little until your skin heals itself." He dug in his saddlebags. "Here it is."

"So whether I was here or at home I would still be itching?"

He handed the bottle over. "You got it."

He applied some of the pink lotion. It felt great going on, and although it didn't bring total relief, it did help. He held the bottle out, but the man shook his head. "No, you keep it, you need it a powerful sight more than I do."

Tony had been toying with the idea of eliminating this witness, but couldn't bring himself to do it now.

The man said, "Sorry I can't let you have my horse, but I'm a long ways from the ranch, and these old legs can't walk that far anymore."

Tony felt warmth for the old man and put the thought of killing him out of his mind, figuring the old fool probably wouldn't be able to describe him very well anyway. "Thank you all the same, but I'm afraid I don't ride, so your horse would not be of much use to me."

"Well," the old man said, swinging up into the saddle. "You got a long walk ahead of you. If you have any more trouble, build you up a fire and put a lot of fresh grass on it so it'll smoke a lot. I'll keep an eye up there and come for you if I see it. If I don't see it, the forest rangers will come if you keep it up for a spell."

Tony nodded as the old man rode off. Forest rangers? He hadn't considered that. Did they carry guns? Were they a threat? He'd better keep his fires small and the smoke down.

◊

"Looks like we underestimated the boy," Little Bear looked down at the empty campsite. It didn't take much for him to pick up the man's trail or follow it until it crossed the stream. "Looks like he's trying the trail in reverse. Maybe it'll look better to him that way."

The Indian followed along at a trot, stopping suddenly and kneeling down. "He left the trail here, I'd say an hour or so ago." Straightening up, he looked out across the valley. "How are your eyes, little brother?"

"Fair, I guess."

"Then take the binoculars and keep sweeping ahead of us. You be my far eyes and I shall keep my eyes on the ground, working out his trail. Your job is to keep us from running up on him."

"You got it."

They started off, Little Bear sensitive to bent grass, scuffs on rocks, occasional tracks in the dirt, working out the trail methodically and effectively. He kept up a reasonable walking pace.

They hadn't gone far before Wayne said, "Somebody's coming."

Little Bear's head snapped up and he watched as the figure advanced. Even without the glasses, he said, "That would be old man Wilson. He's one of the hands on this ranch. They call him Wee Willie."

"Why?"

"They like the sound of it, I guess."

Little Bear held up his hand, palm out as the horse approached. "*Yatahey*, Willie, peace be with you."

"Hello, Little Bear. Who you got with you?"

"This is Wayne Tunnell, Buck's cousin."

The two shook hands as the old man said, "I saw your pigeon back over at the tank. He asked me where Buck's cabin was. I told him I didn't know for sure, but I sent him up to the old abandoned line shack."

Little Bear chuckled. "That's about as far away from Buck's cabin as he can get and still be on the ranch."

"Yeah, that's what I figured. I did have to give him some calamine lotion, though."

Little Bear grimaced, "Sorry to hear that."

The old man laughed and slapped his knee. "Yeah, I figured you did it to him, but I was a little worried about him realizing I could identify him. I figured I had better make him realize he might need a friend out here."

"That's good thinking, my friend. He's quite capable of deciding to eliminate witnesses."

"That's what worried me. Course I got a good look at him." The old man folded his work gloves and put them in his pocket.

"You need to warn all the other hands about where he is and tell them to stay away from him. They might not be so lucky."

"Thought I would. You headed after him?"

"We aim to keep tabs on him. He hasn't been any threat yet and may not be if I can work him right. Of course, I can put him down if it becomes necessary, but I don't believe in taking a life or even wounding a man unless I have no alternative."

"Well, the guy was mighty polite and mighty friendly, but he didn't smile with his eyes, only his mouth. Were I you, I wouldn't give him no edge. I'd say he was big time dangerous."

"Thank you, my friend, I do not underestimate him."

"Well, he underestimates us. Why do you suppose it is all Yankees think we're stupid because we talk slower than they do?"

"It's simply the way things are, but it's often useful, is it not?"

"Nearly always, Little Bear, nearly always. " The old man rode off laughing.

Chapter 22

It was almost dark when Tony found the line shack. He could tell from quite some distance it was deserted and immediately began to regret the decision to not kill the old man. He just might have to go back and do it before he left.

Cabin was too fancy a word for the three-sided lean-to. Still, it broke the wind and had a couple of rope-sprung cots and a fireplace. The best part was that stack of firewood already cut. Tony poked around in a little cupboard and found a couple of cans of beans, two pots, and, wonder of wonders, a couple of rolls of toilet paper.

He crossed himself for his good fortune, finishing with a touch to his lips with his fingers. Shock came into his eyes as he realized what he had done. He sure hoped that poison wouldn't spread any further.

He looked at the toilet paper. All those years he had taken this wonderful material for granted. Never again. After he made a little fire, he went out to a makeshift outhouse to treat his painfully sore bottom to this magical paper and a little lotion.

◊

Little Bear sat in the brush, studying the lean-to as he decided what to do with this new situation. He had prevailed upon Wee Willie to double up and take Wayne back to Buck's cabin. As he chewed a piece of jerky, he imagined the good food Wayne would be eating about now.

While the other man had meditated in the latrine, Little Bear worked a slow circle around the area to see what he might be able to use. By the end of his investigation, the man had returned to the shack.

The latrine was nothing more than a small trench with a crude log seat fashioned over it, used with your business end suspended between the two logs. Little Bear took his hunting knife and deeply notched the two logs in the middle on the bottom side.

Little Bear slipped back into the woods where his prey would be upwind of him and unwrapped a little slab of bacon. He made a hat sized fire back under some overhanging foliage which hid what little smoke the fire produced and cooked some bacon for a sandwich. He saved the bacon grease in the little pan.

When he got back to the lean-to, he saw that the man had arranged what was left of his sleeping bag on the cot and had apparently gone immediately to sleep. Once he was breathing deeply enough to suit Little Bear, the Indian went a short distance back in the woods to an animal den he had found and left little drops of warm bacon grease in a trail back to the lean-to.

He knew bacon grease would draw animals like catnip would draw a cat. Even animals who didn't eat bacon would attracted by the delicious smelling scent. In minutes, small, furry, black-and-white striped kitties were all over the small enclosure. Little Bear flipped a pebble on the sleeping form to wake him. Tony's sleepy eyes opened a mere slit to find another pair of eyes at the opposite end of his nose. Sniffing curiously at the man were a mama skunk and three... no, four babies.

Little Bear grinned. He figured the man wouldn't be smart enough to lie there and let them leave. He'd be sorely disappointed if that happened.

Okay. Looked like even a city boy knew a skunk when he saw one, and his reflexes took over the moment he came full awake. He jerked back from the animal. By then it was too late to hold still. Skunks have very poor vision, and the sudden move scared the mama. She bought time for her babies to escape in the only way nature provided.

The man had no time to escape. That mama hosed the entire cot and him as well with the foulest smelling spray God in his infinite wisdom ever saw fit to place on this earth. The man fought to get a breath as he staggered outside to collapse.

Little Bear held his laughter with great difficulty. It was too dark to see, but the Indian figured the man's complexion was sure to be colored a subtle, but definite shade of green.

Little Bear was also sure the man's evening would be busy, so he'd best get himself back to Buck's cabin to re-provision. He was about to leave when the man started to get sick. Little Bear watched him stagger to the outhouse and lean on the makeshift seat to throw up. The seat gave way at the notches, and the man went head first down into the latrine.

Little Bear shook his head. "Not how I planned it, but I guess one end is as good as the other." He smiled, "maybe better,"

After he got far enough away, he reported in to Buck by radio.

"I'll heat up some grub," Buck said. "Willie took a horse for you, left it by the windmill."

"Glad not to have to walk the whole way back." Little Bear

would owe Willie for that good deed.

◊

At first light the next morning, Buck shook Wayne awake. "I'm going with Little Bear this time. I want you here with Junior. There are two shotguns, a double barrel twelve gauge and a twelve gauge pump leaning by the door." He paused for emphasis. "They *are* loaded, and there's a shell in the chamber. I don't want either of you out in the open, do you understand? I think we're going to keep this guy occupied, but there's no reason to take any chances."

Little Bear was already mounted when Buck swung into the saddle, then turned his horse in behind Little Bear's. It didn't take them long to find their quarry's smoke signals.

They tied the horses and completed the distance on foot, coming in on the uphill side so they could lie there and look down on him. The man had a fire going out in the open. Buck looked through the binoculars. "He's burning his bedroll... and looks like some clothes."

"Small wonder," Little Bear said.

"I wonder if he can hold anything on his stomach yet."

Little Bear took his turn with the binoculars. "Depends. Do you suppose he knows to wash with tomato juice?"

Buck smiled. "Even if he did, you think he carried any up here?"

"Well, he'll get used to the smell to some extent, particularly when he gets some fresh clothes on."

Buck made a distasteful expression. "If it were me, I'd make me a smoky fire and stand in the smoke for as long as I could stand

144

it."

"Yes, it would help, but I doubt he knows that trick, either."

Buck clucked his tongue. "Look at him, throwing stuff around. If he was dangerous to begin with, he's a loose cannon now."

Little Bear rolled over to look at Buck. "Maybe we should get the drop on him and arrest him."

"On what charge?"

He put the glasses down. "What charge? We know he's here to attempt murder."

"Knowing and proving are not the same. Nothing would happen to him. We'd just postpone the inevitable, and he would come back better prepared next time. But it doesn't sit well with me to just sit back and wait for him to take a shot at Junior."

"No, I still hope to break him and cause him to quit. However, worst case, we can wait until he actually tries to position himself to shoot and take him then."

"Yeah, that would be proof enough."

"We wouldn't need proof, only enough to convince our conscience, for we could take no chances at such a point. I would have to take him down, and I could not risk trying merely to wound him."

Buck nodded somberly. He knew Little Bear was right.

"But perhaps it won't come to that." Buck looked at the picture of utter frustration down below them. "This man has to be near his breaking point."

"Lord knows, in his shoes, I would be," Little Bear said.

◊

When the stranger packed up his diminishing supply of gear and headed toward the hilltop, Buck had to hustle to move the horses under cover. He watched as the man looked around and then headed off. Smack toward his cabin.

"Oh, this isn't good" he said.

The path took the man over one ridge after another. Buck saw him stagger, his shoulders sagging, until he stopped for lunch. He made a small fire to heat water, gulped a few bites, then fell asleep.

Buck turned as Little Bear approached and said, "It is too early, we can't let him sleep yet. We need him in this exhausted state."

"Any ideas?"

"Maybe." Like a ghost, Little Bear slipped down to the man's camp. He picked up a burning stick out of the fire and put it under the man's back pack, positioning it so the flashlight clipped to the outside of the pack sat directly on the embers.

Flames had begun to lick around the pack when the batteries in the flashlight exploded. Tony came to his feet with the rifle in his hands. He saw the burning pack and started throwing dirt on it.

He removed the burning branch and stared at it, cursing. "Stupid thing must have popped out of the fire." He inspected the damage. "What else could possibly happen in this god-forsaken place?"

Buck and Little Bear grinned at each other. The man managed to stuff what was left of his gear in his pack, before starting up the ridge again.

Little Bear pointed to the rattlesnake rattles and then to the path. Buck nodded, understanding lighting his eyes. No sooner had

Little Bear started shaking these, than the man changed course again. He had to repeat the exercise a few more times, but by doing so kept the stranger away from the cabin.

When the man set up camp for the night, he wasn't much closer than he had been at daybreak.

◊

Little Bear tucked the rattles back in his own pack and asked, "Have you ever seen anybody as stubborn as this guy?"

"Outside of yourself, you mean?"

"Well, I think it is time to put an end to it."

"You have something in mind?" Buck glanced over his shoulder at the trail behind. He'd sure like it to end so he could get on with other things in his life. Much as he loved his cabin, there were things needed tending to in town.

"I do, but I will need a diversion." Little Bear nodded toward the man's camp. "Remember those deer we saw in the clearing? When he starts fixing food, I need you to get your horse and see if you can chase one of them close enough to get his attention without letting him see you."

"Sure thing."

Deer couldn't be herded like cows, but Buck managed to chase them in such a manner that he had not one, but five deer headed toward the fool's camp. They made quite a noise as they bounded through the brush. The man picked up his rifle. At the edge of the light, he strained to see out into the darkness.

Suddenly, all five deer burst from the thicket at the same time and nearly got themselves shot before the man lowered his gun.

Little Bear approached while the man had his back to the fire and dropped a handful of something in the water. Buck figured Little Bear had things under control, so he headed back up to meet him.

From their lookout point, they heard the man speak as he scooped up a trail meal "If I ever get out of this place, I'm never going outdoors again. I may not even mow the yard anymore."

Buck eyed Little Bear. "So, are you going to tell me what you put in his water, or what?"

"Peyote."

"Peyote. That stuff is illegal."

"So go arrest him. He's using it, not me."

"Is that what you have in mind?"

"No, I think something better may come of it."

Buck's eye brows shot up. "Doesn't it make a person hallucinate?"

"Oh, does it ever."

The hit man no longer had a bedroll, so he had to build up the fire and curl up next to it.

While they waited for the potion to take effect, Little Bear stripped to the waist and used some clay and charcoal to make war paint all over his face and body. Buck watched in wonder. "I'm afraid to ask what it is you're doing."

"It's just as well."

◊

Something hit Tony hard and rolled him over on his back. His eyes came open, but everything appeared fuzzy and streaked with vivid colors. His mind grappled with the fact that there seemed to be a rather large Indian with bright markings sitting right in the middle of his chest. This apparition drove stakes into the ground and was tying Tony's wrists to them. The flickering firelight made the colors even more hideous and ghostly. What was happening?

He wanted to move, but lethargy gripped him as the figure moved to tie his ankles as well. He should be resisting, but his muscles didn't respond to what felt like a random thought. He was outside of his body watching the events with only a mild interest.

"Are you an Indian?" he asked as the form looked down at him.

"I am the spirit of Wa-na-hona, warrior chief of the Deer clan. You trespass on sacred land."

"I did not...I didn't see any signs." He still felt no fear. Perhaps he should, but that too seemed of only minor interest.

The figure finished tying his ankles and suddenly was right in his face. "You did not see me, either, but I was there. I sent a water sign against you telling you to leave my land, but you heeded it not."

"You...sent the water?"

The apparition stood up. "Then I sent a legion of snakes to drive you from my land," he made a large sweeping gesture, "but you heard not the cries of their forked tongues."

"Nobody... can... send snakes..." The memory of the snakes filtered through the haze. The snakes were horrible. Could someone have commanded them? This puzzled Tony.

"No one can send skunk or deer either, yet they came."

"How...how do you know all of this?"

"You say there were no signs. I say the signs were many but you paid no mind."

Tony glanced to the right, staring at his hand at the stake. "Why? Why am I tied up?" The question seemed quite clear to him. So why wasn't the answer just as clear?

The apparition again got right in his face and spoke with an exaggerated slowness. "There are many possible penalties for violating our sacred land. I intend to scalp you, then if you live long enough, skin you."

Tony's heart sped at the Indian's words. Scalp him? Skin him? His eyes rounded, but all he could do was emit a yelp.

The Indian pulled himself up into a haughty pose. "I am a spirit, who is to stop me?" The Indian seemed to have read his mind. Tony slammed shut his eyes, hoping the image would disappear. It didn't. Instead, the Indian said, "Besides, your soul is black. You are a killer of men. No one will sing death songs in your lodge."

"How... " Tony felt his breath stop momentarily. A lump formed in his throat, threatening to choke him. "You can't know...anything."

"All is known in the spirit world."

◊

Suddenly, Little Bear knelt, grabbed a handful of the man's hair, cut it off with a razor sharp knife. It was only hair, but in the man's present state of mind, he saw much more. His eyes widened even more.

Little Bear spun to look into the darkness, "Yes, my father?"

He stood as if listening. "But this one does not deserve to live, great one." Still he listened to the darkness, then he looked down saying, "My Chief says I must give you another chance."

Beads of sweat dripped off the man's face, glistening in the firelight. "I didn't hear anything."

Little Bear ignored the comment. "I give you until the sun is over the trees. If you are still on my land then, I will hunt you, and I shall finish this." He held the handful of hair in the man's face.

The man gulped, whimpering. "How far does your land go?"

"The sacred land is where my animals live, where my trees grow strong and straight. I may not leave the sanctity of the forest."

Little Bear saw the relief as it flooded the man. He could almost smell it.

"No problem. Unless you hunt and skin taxicabs, I'll be off your land."

Using his knife, Little Bear sliced through the man's shirt and pants. "You may keep your underpants and your shoes. That is all. At the bottom of this hill you will find a stream. Follow the flow of the water, and it will take you where you need to go. You had best start or the sun will give you to me. Go," Little Bear said, as he cut the cord on the man's right wrist, "for my knife is thirsty, and it hopes you will not make it."

He gathered up the man's pack and the rifle and disappeared as silently as he had come.

It took the man over ten minutes to free his left hand and his ankles. He stumbled some as he hurried to follow Little Bear's orders and fell in the stream several times.

Buck handed Little Bear his shirt. "No academy award for that."

"No? He look like he's scared to you?"

"It must have been the special effects, because it certainly wasn't the acting."

Little Bear swiped at his painted skin and asked, with a hint of derision in his voice, "Have you ever come face to face with a genuine Indian spirit?"

Buck grinned. "Can't say I have."

"Then don't critique what you don't understand."

"Think it's worth our time to follow this guy?"

"Never leave a job half finished." Little Bear gathered his things. "Besides, I've got one last little shot in mind."

"Really?"

"Yeah, you know the canyon just before he'll get back to his car?"

"That's Yellow Ridge Canyon, isn't it?"

"There's a very nice little echo there."

"Ah ha."

"I intend to cup my hands and yell... the spirits have smiled on you, white eyes. You have made it in time... but never return... never... I shall be waiting!" Buck shook his head. "Now see, that's what I was talking about. Who's going to believe that? It's overacting and seriously corny."

"We'll see how corny it is when we watch how fast he drives down the road."

Chapter 23

Junior and Wayne leaned forward to listen as Little Bear related the story. Light glowed from the fireplace.

Junior threw his head back and laughed. "Little Bear, I don't know how to thank you. This is the first time I've felt relaxed in years." Then his smile faded. "Of course, it's only temporary, they'll send somebody else."

"Maybe. Maybe not," Little Bear said.

Junior raised his cup. "At any rate, it won't be anytime soon."

Buck joined the laughter. "And it won't be anybody who talks to that guy!."

"How did you get into all of this, Mr. Jorgenson," Wayne leaned back in his chair.

"It's Junior, son, everybody calls me Junior." He took a sip of coffee as he looked into the fire. "You know, people make mistakes in their lives and they have to pay for them. They fall in with the wrong people, or marry the wrong person, or do something stupid. In my case, I didn't do anything but look out of a window at the wrong time."

He paused to sip again. "You see, I finally figured out I was getting too old to rodeo and tried my hand working in my Uncle's butcher shop in Queens. One day, I looked out a window to see Ralph DeGrassi pull the plug on a guy. This guy was on his knees begging for his life, but DeGrassi was as cool as a cucumber. One chance glance out of a window changed my whole life."

Wayne nodded "What had the guy done?"

"From what I could hear through the window, he seems to have broken their so-called code. These guys throw around words like code, honor, respect, and family and it makes what they do sound very high falutin and honorable. But there's nothing honorable about murder and drugs."

"So you testified against him?"

"Yes, and he got life. So now they hunt for me."

Wayne shook his head. "I don't understand. It looks like it would have been over and done with when he went to jail."

"No, you don't understand how these guys think. They have a contract out on me, not because I can hurt him any further, but because people can't be allowed to think they can harm the organization and get away with it."

"I still don't see," Little Bear said, "If he's locked up and going to stay locked up, why does it matter?"

Jack laughed. "The way the mob thinks they figured they'd have people testifying against them all over the place. This fear is what keeps people in line. So you see, they don't care how long it takes, they have to get it done."

"So you went into the witness protection program?"

Junior nodded. "Yes, but the mob's resources are amazing. They bribe some clerk or utilize this world-wide network of criminals, and the next thing you know, they're breathing down your neck again."

"And you came back here so strangers would be easier to spot?"

"Yes, and it looked like it worked." He frowned. "Of course, I can't keep doing it because it puts too many of my friends in danger.

Buck shook his head, "No, the principle is good. We do need to see if we can find a way to refine the idea a bit. Let's not be in any big hurry to send you back off into oblivion again. We can always fort up here again if need be."

"We'll see, but I don't like the idea of other people fighting my battles for me."

Little Bear grinned. "You would take this fun from me? I haven't enjoyed myself so much in years."

◊

Raul stood in the door of Buck's office and waited for him to get off the phone. As he hung up he said, "What is it?"

"Have a couple of missing cattle reports this morning."

"The cattlemen's barbecue coming up?"

"Saturday."

Buck winked. "So, what else is new? These guys only report them stolen to aggravate each other."

"But it makes work for us."

"No, it's simply playing the game. You have to admit the food we'll get Saturday is ample pay."

Raul rubbed his stomach, "You got that right. I can hardly wait."

"What else?"

The big deputy shrugged. "Well, I have a little bad news. Jim Minor has filed to run against you for sheriff."

"He's a good man."

155

"Yeah, we've been talking about it, so I filed to run as well to dilute any impact he might have. That way, with us splitting up the vote, your regular vote should put you back in easy."

"I appreciate the thought, though I'm not sure I agree with your logic."

"What do you mean?"

Buck pushed back in his chair, "Raul, this town is better than 30% Hispanic. If you get their vote, it could carry you into office easy."

"You really think so?" Raul looked utterly amazed.

"Sure."

"I'll pull out then. It wasn't my intention to be up against you for real."

"No, don't pull out. It may be your time, and time for me to call it quits. I'll tell you what I'll do. You run your best race, and I will as well. Whoever gets the job will hire the other as his chief deputy."

Raul looked amazed. "You could work as my deputy?"

"Sure, I've got this friend over in New Mexico who works in a county where the sheriff can't win succeeding terms, so he and his chief deputy take turns being sheriff and chief deputy. I don't see why we can't do it if they can."

"I don't know. I'll have to think about that."

"You mean you wouldn't want me as a deputy?" Buck gave him an amused look.

"No, that's not it. I've learned everything I know from you. I don't think I could take the top job."

Buck shook his head. "Don't think of it that way. Think of it

156

as taking on more responsibility so I can kick back a little. You'd be doing me a favor. Don't worry, I'm not going to roll over on the deal. I'll do my best, and if you get the job, it'll be because people want you."

By the time Buck got home to the porch in the evening, the group was assembled, including Junior. From the look on Raul's face, he was still wrestling with the problem. Barney made matters worse: "Well, look here. We got two of the three candidates in the sheriff's race right here. Why don't we invite Minor over, and we can have our own candidate forum right here on the porch."

Buck cut in. "Now lay off, Barney. Raul isn't too comfortable with this notion right now, and he doesn't deserve to get hassled about it."

Doc cut in sharply. "Then what did he do it for? He was merely an unemployed local when you hired him."

Raul looked crestfallen. "Exactly what's bothering me, Doc. I feel like I'm biting the hand that feeds me. I thought I was doing Buck a favor, splitting up the vote so Buck could take Minor easy."

"Minor's no threat," Doc said. "Never has been."

"That's what Buck said, but he says the Hispanic vote might be."

"Now, there's a fact, what with the three of you splitting up the Anglo vote. You go and get the Hispanic vote on top of that, and it could be a winning combination."

Buck said, "Now you guys back off. If Raul's got the votes, then he deserves the office. That's how it works. Don't worry, we've cut a deal. The winner gets to wear the badge and the other gets to be chief deputy, no matter which way it goes."

"You could do that?" Barney asked with disbelief in his voice.

"Are you kidding? Set back and let somebody else take the heat for a while? Man, it would be like getting to retire, but with a paycheck coming in. I could spend more time out at the church."

Barney said, "I got to hand it to you, Buck, you're amazing."

"No, the only one who's amazing around here is the big Indian sitting next to you. You heard the story about what happened up at the cabin yet?"

"Wayne told us, in great detail," Doc said

"Well, I've got to tell you it was incredible how he handled the guy, but I sure wish you could have seen his bad acting as he did it. I can't believe the jerk bought it."

Little Bear's brows lowered. You're going to take this thing too far, Buck."

"Now don't get testy on us, Chief. When an actor gives a performance, he has to be strong enough to face the reviews the following morning."

Little Bear opened his mouth, but Wayne beat him to it. "You know, Buck, I know you're only having fun with Little Bear. But I gotta say his stuff sounded real to me."

"What did?"

"Haven't you ever seen Scrooge? The ghosts of Christmas past, present, and future? They talked really weird and real formal, and all of these shows I see where some spirit comes to counsel somebody? They always talk very big-g-g," he said, making an expanding gesture with his hands, "and they always talk in this kind of very proper, extravagant voice. If I was a spirit, I think it's how I'd talk."

Little Bear smirked. "You see what I was going for, Buck? Perhaps my performance did lack something to make it credible, or perhaps your credentials as a critic should be in question."

Doc chuckled. "It appears to me the person in the best position to critique this performance would be the man it was aimed at. How about if we ask him?"

Buck threw his head back and laughed. "Now, I'd admire to do it, Doc, only he ain't stopped running yet. He didn't even turn his rent car back in, but abandoned it outside of Dallas. I don't know where he went from there, but it's far, Doc, it's real far."

Junior got up and picked up an empty can from beside his chair. "Well, I think those actions speak louder than anything anybody's said so far. I declare it an Academy Award performance." He turned to Little Bear and held out the can. "I hereby present you with this here major award being as how I'm the person who benefited most from its presentation."

Little Bear took it somberly. "I accept with great humility and shall treasure it always."

Seeing a great opening, Buck opened his mouth, but changed his mind. "I can see this joke has gone far enough." He lifted his beverage in salute. "I concur. You did great."

"Well, before we get plumb sloppy sentimental, what are we going to do with the next one?" asked Junior.

Doc's head popped up. "Next one?"

Junior folded himself back in his chair. It was his turn to look dejected. "Yes, the next one. Like we said, they'll keep coming until they get me. I don't want anybody else getting hurt, so I'm going to call the Feds and get hidden out again."

Buck shook his head. "No, I don't agree. Your instinct about us being able to spot newcomers in a small town was a good one. Besides, here you have help."

"At least, if they got to me here, I'd be going out among friends. I know once you're dead it doesn't matter, but the thought of my body lying in an empty church bothers me more than the thought of getting killed. Besides, here I know you'd preach a whale of a funeral."

"I would indeed, but let's not be thinking that way. Only, we've got to have a new plan. We can't count on the same thing working twice."

"I have thought on this," Little Bear said, "and it would seem to me they would seek to send someone next time who could perform out in the wild country."

"All the more reason for me to leave," Junior still looked worried.

Little Bear shook his head. "No, the cabin is still the safest place in the entire world to deal with them, even if they send someone at home in that kind of country. The trick is knowing he's here, 'cause he wouldn't stick out like ones so far have done."

"But he'd still be a stranger," Buck said. "Out here they'll always be a stranger no matter who they send."

Barney looked like he didn't buy it, "I hate to bring this up, but I don't think you could count on that."

"What are you talking about?"

"It's a sad commentary, Buck, but for the right money, somebody could be bought. Even right here among people we know."

Buck frowned. "That's a hard thing to say."

"Yes it is, but you know it's true. Still, the likelihood is much greater for it to be someone from the outside."

Chapter 24

Ralph DeGrassi prided himself on having come up the hard way to his present position as a kingpin of organized crime. His dark features showed the marks of physical combat. Even here he held sway because so many of his former soldiers lodged here with him, besides all the people who curried his favor in anticipation of their release. Even the guards accorded him a more elevated status. The guards knew he could cause trouble--or quell it.

At visiting time, Degrassi followed the guard to the common room to meet with Victor Greggs, a Lieutenant on the outside and a loyal subordinate. Victor hesitatingly reported on the failure of the gunman.

DeGrassi said, "This, I do not like to hear. You told me this guy was the best."

"He was the best here in New York, but his mark went up into the mountains. You ought to talk to the guy, Mr. DeGrassi. He raves on about snakes, wild Indians, and unspeakable things. He ain't no good no more, sir. He's a beaten man."

"This thing cannot be allowed to stand," Degrassi's voice was hoarse from suppressed emotion. "We must redeem our honor. Someone else must be sent."

"There's lots of guys who can go, Boss, but I think something different is called for. I think sending anyone else who isn't at home up in those mountains would be a mistake."

"This makes sense. Where do we find a mountain man these days?"

"I'll ask around, Boss, but you might oughta put the word out in here. There's lots of different type guys here in stir."

DeGrassi nodded, "If somebody is in here, it won't take long to find out. you get back to me, in a couple of days, you hear?"

The word went out through the prison, and a couple of hours later two of DeGrassi's goons escorted a young man to him out in the exercise yard. "Mr. DeGrassi, this guy wants to talk to you."

"Who are you?" Degrassi glared at the man. He had sandy hair, was slim as a street lamp and looked as much like a redneck as anything he had ever seen.

"I'm Lee Bob Courtland."

"What are you in for?"

"Tax evasion, but it boils down to moonshining."

Degrassi made a dismissive gesture. "Moonshining went out with prohibition."

"No, it's true there ain't much of it anymore, but there's still a little money to be made if you don't have to pay those taxes on what you make."

"You got something for me?"

Courtland said, "Word is, you're looking for someone who can hunt and can hunt up in the mountains."

Degrassi was interested now. "You know someone like this?"

Courtland jerked a finger toward his chest. "Me! I get out in two weeks, and I can track a varmint up a brick wall. I'm a good shot, too."

"They tell you where this guy is holed up?"

"Yes, sir, but mountains is mountains. I could get it done for you."

"It's worth 25 G's if you can, plus expenses. If you can't, then someone will be looking for you instead."

Lee Bob gulped. "Yes, sir, I understand, but I ain't ever seen that much money all at one time. I reckon I gotta give it a try."

◊

Raul walked up on the porch. "Looks like your boy's here."

"What do you have?" Buck asked.

"Some guy who's so country he doesn't even seem to be comfortable wearing shoes is holed up out at the Hutton House, spending money like he hasn't ever seen it before. All the merchants downtown are talking about it. He's another one putting out a neon sign."

Buck looked down, considering this information. "We had best not underestimate him. He sounds like what we were afraid of. I think somebody who doesn't know how to act in town, particularly a major metropolitan area like Clear Creek, is probably right at home out in the woods."

Barney agreed, "If that's true, why don't you reverse your strategy and fort up here in town?"

Buck nodded, "I was thinking on the same thing, Barney. One thing for sure, we don't want to play into his hands. Junior, how do you feel about sleeping up in the jail for a few days while we take this guy's measure?"

"Won't be the first time. Be the first time I ever went in sober, though."

Buck grinned, "Well, you've still got time to correct that if it bothers you."

"I reckon not."

"Where's Little Bear?" Doc asked.

Raul turned to face him. "He's been on this guy since mid-afternoon. I expect he knows what kind of underwear the guy is partial to by now."

Buck looked at Raul. "First time we catch this guy out of his room, get a glass he's been handling and let's get some prints. I'll bet the ranch he has a record."

"Sure, I can do that," Raul said. "Or I can give you this rap sheet, if you'd rather."

"What?"

Raul shrugged. "Buck, what can I tell you? The guy checked in under his right name."

"You're kidding."

"Why would I kid about something like that?" Raul pulled out a sheet. "His name is Lee Bob Courtland, and he comes from the mountains of Tennessee. He did time for tax evasion, specifically for not paying the tax on whiskey his family seems to be partial to making. It seems to be his only brush with the law."

"Sounds like he's dumb as dogfood, but I still say he's probably able to move in the woods like a cat."

"No bet there," Raul said.

Raul's belt radio crackled to life, and Little Bear's voice came in. "It looks like our pigeon is settling in the nest for the night. Should I sit on him?"

Buck held out his hand, and Raul gave him the mike. "Little

Bear, this is Buck, I'm sending a night patrol unit over to do stakeout. You come back over here, and I'm going to buy you a big, old steak."

"Does it have to be an old steak?"

"Your choice, but they're better if they're aged."

◊

Lee Bob Courtland was living in unabashed splendor for the first time in his life, and the seduction had begun with filling out the little card where you could order your breakfast and they would bring it right to the room at the hour you wished. Can you imagine that? *Right to the room!*

A knock on the door signaled its arrival and Lee Bob opened it to find a young man with a tray.

"Your breakfast, sir."

"Ain't that something? I never had nobody fetch it to me before, lessen you count the time Mama brought it in when I had the chicken pox."

"Ah... yes sir, will you have it over at the table?"

Lee Bob's eyebrows raised. "Where else would you have it?"

"Some people have it in bed, sir."

"In bed?" The concept completely escaped Lee Bob. "Do I pay you?"

"You can merely sign your ticket, sir, and it will be put on your bill. Of course, there is generally the matter of a gratuity."

"What's a grat... what you said?"

"It's a tip, sir. People usually give a waiter a tip for good service."

"A tip?"

"Yes, sir, a small amount of money to insure they continue to get good service."

He looked confused. "If I don't pay extra, I don't get good service?"

"Oh no, sir, it's not like that at all. You'll get good service anyway. People usually give a tip to show their gratitude for it, that's all."

"What's gratitude?"

The bellman looked haughty. "When people are treated nice by those who wait on them, they generally show they are happy by giving a little tip."

"Well, I sure want to do what's right, how little?"

It was the bellman's turn to lift his eyebrows. "Generally about 35%."

"I'm not much for ciphering, how do I know how much that is?"

"Your check is $9.48, sir, the tip would be roughly four dollars. You can just add it to the bill when you sign it."

Lee Bob passed it over and grinned sheepishly. "I reckon I'm a little country. I don't get into the city much."

"I'm here to serve, sir, if you need anything at all, you ask for Dave."

Lee Bob had turned to go to his breakfast, but he stopped and turned back. "Like what?"

"If you order lunch or dinner, or need a bottle, or, well,... shall I say companionship, or simply need to know where to find anything. You just ask for me personally."

"You can have meals besides breakfast brought to you?"

"Yes, sir, there's a menu in the desk."

"Don't that beat all?" Then it registered. "What do you mean companionship?"

Dave leered, "You know, sir, a woman."

"You can order up women like a meal?"

"Not everyone can get it done for you, sir, but I can."

Lee Bob scratched the back of his head. What is the world coming to? "What would this woman do, clean up the place?"

"No, sir, a housekeeper will come and do that and make the bed."

This was all so confusing. "Am I supposed to tip her?"

"Yes, Sir, it's customary. You give it to me and I see that she gets it."

"Don't that beat all? what do you rent this woman for if somebody else is going to do the cleaning?"

Dave clearly didn't believe it, this guy was serious. "Haven't you ever had a woman, sir?"

"I ain't never been married. Wait a minute, are you talking about a *harlot*"

"Well, they prefer to be known as escorts, sir."

Lee Bob was indignant. "Well, I don't hold with that kind of stuff. My mama would skin me alive. I'm beginning to kinda wonder about you, too, Dave, if you're suggesting such a thing."

"Oh, no, sir, I don't approve myself, only a lot of gentlemen do. I simply have to make sure they know it's available."

The frown erased from his face. "Well, I don't want you to ever mention it again." He perked up. "I could use me a bottle though, do they make a tolerable shine hereabouts?"

"Shine, sir?"

"Yeah, moonshine, you know, white lightning?"

Dave shook his head vigorously. "No, sir, I don't think anybody makes that around here.

"They make it where I come from," Lee Bob said. "Lot of mountain folks have quite a taste for it."

"I could get you a bottle of Everclear. I suspect it's the closest to it we'd have."

Any port in a storm, "Okay, I'll give it a shot. Do I give you the money to do it?"

"Yes, sir."

"Do I give you the tip for it now or when you come back?"

"You give me the money for it, but tips are always after service is delivered, sir."

Lee Bob got his wallet and handed over the money. "Well, Dave, if you're gonna work with me, there's one other thing we gotta clear up."

"Yes, sir?"

"We didn't even lay a 'sir' on our daddy. It makes me a mite uncomfortable for you to keep doing it to me. My name is Lee Bob."

"Yes, sir, that is... Lee Bob."

"Well, there ain't no hurry on the bottle, you hear. I don't hold with drinking 'til after the sun's started dropping."

"Yes, sir."

"Am I going to have trouble out of you?"

"No, sir, I mean no, Lee Bob."

Chapter 25

Buck paid off on his steak offer at Vernon's Steak House. They went to work on two steaks so large they left little room on the platter for the baked potato. As he sawed off another bite with the steak knife, Buck said, "How do you think we ought to handle this new hit man?"

Little Bear said, "We should take him back up to the cabin."

Buck paused with a bite of steak on his fork. "he's not the same type critter as the last one."

"This I know. I'm looking forward to the challenge. However, if you have no faith in me, we can leave Junior up in the jail and make this man believe he has gone to the cabin."

"It ain't a matter of faith, Chief. I don't think we should risk him. Plus, if you're dead set on doing this, you'd have a lot more freedom to work if there wasn't actually any danger of him getting by you."

"Yes... Yes, there is wisdom in this. We shall do as you say. We shall decoy him up to the mountains and see what he's made of."

"I think we ought to wait until we're sure he's on to where Junior is, then we'll let him see us taking him out and leak the word as to where we're going. Then we'll drop Junior off on the way, and you can lead this guy up there. I'll have Raul meet us to babysit Junior, and I'll go back you up."

"No offense intended, old friend, but I stand a better chance if it is only me and him in the mountains by ourselves."

"I don't like that," Buck said with a frown. "This guy is dangerous."

"I shall take no chance, but I really think he is no great danger to anyone but Junior."

"I don't think you can count on that."

"I don't intend to, but I do think it's true."

◊

Dave arrived with the bottle shortly after Lee Bob returned to his room. The bellman was working days and though he generally stayed around until after six and the bulk of the check-in's had arrived, he was due to be off. He couldn't take a chance on letting one of the other guys get the scent of this pigeon, however. It was too sweet a deal.

He knocked on the door and Lee Bob answered wearing nothing but a towel. "Hey there, Dave boy, come on in. Let me throw on a pair of pants." Dave watched as the tall, lanky frame disappeared into the bathroom. In a moment Lee Bob came back out, rubbing his sandy blonde hair with a towel.

"I can't hardly get enough of that shower. I done been in it three, maybe four times. It feels really great."

"Have you tried the hot tub?" Dave asked.

"No, I ain't got down in the tub. I like the pressure of the water running on me."

"The hot tub is over by the swimming pool."

"You mean take a bath in public?" Lee Bob was incredulous.

"No, sir, it's not a bath. You wear a swimming suit. It's very

171

hot water and it has jets that fill the water with millions of air bubbles. It feels very good, sir."

"Dave, what am I going to have to do to make you quit calling me sir, whomp you?"

"The hotel makes me do it to all the visitors. If they heard me calling you by your proper name, I'd get in trouble."

"I don't want to get you in no trouble, so you do what you have to. Now let's get back to all these air bubbles."

"If you like the shower, trust me, you'd love the hot tub."

"I ain't got one of them swimming suits."

"Give me five minutes, sir." Dave turned to go out. He stopped. "Oh, here's your bottle, sir."

Lee Bob took it and broke the seal. He turned it up to take a big swig. Everclear is very close to being pure grain alcohol. Dave cringed as he watched. "I didn't know anyone drank that straight."

Lee Bob wiped his mouth with the back of his hand. "Well, it ain't got the taste of good corn squeezings, but it has a tolerable bite." He held it out. "Have a little taste?"

Dave held up his hand. "It's a little early for me. I'll be right back with the suit."

"What time you get off?"

"Actually, I'm off now," Dave looked at his watch.

"Why don't you get a suit and come with me? I'd like to visit with you a bit. I'd buy your supper."

"I don't suppose there would be any harm in that."

It took little more than the five minutes promised for Dave to do as promised. Five more and they were comfortably situated in the hot tub. They had the place to themselves.

Lee Bob was weaned on moonshine and even the powerful drink in the plastic glass had little effect on him. Dave, however, was already feeling it. "Man," he said, "I'm surprised this stuff isn't eating right through this plastic glass."

"You were right about this hot tub, it feels really fine," Lee Bob said with a wide grin. "It's kinda like this hot spring we got up in the mountains over to goat holler way, makes a body feel real good."

"Well, it's about to get better."

"How so?"

"Look what's coming." Dave pointed with a nod of his head.

Headed their way were two young ladies in very brief bikinis. Lee Bob gulped, "Lord a mighty, that's as little as I ever saw anybody have on without being plumb buck naked. Are they coming here?"

"I think so."

The girls said, "Mind if we join you? I'm Cathy and this is Carolyn."

Lee Bob stood up. "My name is Lee Bob Courtland and this here is Dave, he works at this place." Dave didn't get up. It is doubtful at this point whether he could if he wanted to. He did wave his glass in an offhand fashion and manage to leer suggestively.

When the girls were seated, Lee Bob sat back down. "I could get to like this here public bathing. Are you girls traveling?"

They giggled and Cathy said, "We're college students on our way back out to California, we go to UCLA."

"You see what?"

"UCLA, it's the name of our school."

He didn't understand, but his attention was diverted as something else registered on him. "You girls sure do look a lot alike."

They giggled again and Carolyn said, "We're twins." At least Lee Bob thought it was Carolyn who said it.

Dave said, "There is a God."

Lee Bob shot him a scornful look, "Twins, well I'll be. I ain't never seen twins before; not human ones, anyways. Old man Tucker's cow had twins once, but I reckon that ain't near as much of a wonderment as twin girls. 'Specially when they're as pretty as you two."

"Thank you, kind sir, are you going to offer us a drink?"

"If you'd like. Our womenfolk up in the mountains generally don't take much to this stuff. They're generally more attuned to a little elderberry wine or the like."

"What is it?"

"Everclear," Dave belched, weaving discernibly.

"Straight? I've had it in a punch before, but never straight. I didn't know anyone ever did that."

"Well, Daniel Boone here thinks it tastes a lot like the moonshine from back home," Dave said sarcastically. "He likes it."

"Dave, where I come from we don't take the name of Colonel Boone lightly. He throws a mighty tall shadow back in the hills."

"Lee Bob, the man is dead." Dave accentuated the statement with his hands.

"What happened to the sir?"

174

"I'm off work now. Anyway, I didn't mean to offend you."

"No one could be offended by being compared to Daniel Boone, or Davy Crockett either, for that matter."

"Yeah, that would be my next choice, all right."

The girls got a couple of plastic glasses and held them out. Cathy said, "I guess we would try a little taste, but only a little one, all right?"

The bottle was illegally by the pool, wrapped in a towel. He poured them about two fingers in the bottom of the glass and refreshed his own drink. He didn't give Dave any more. Dave didn't even notice.

The girls tried a sip and one said, "Oh my! That's like drinking lighter fluid."

"I wouldn't know," Lee Bob said. "I ain't never tried drinking no lighter fluid."

They settled back. Carolyn purred, "It does leave you with a warm feeling in your tummy, though."

Dave said, "It leaves me feeling warm all over, if I had any feeling, that is. Which I don't." He tried his suggestive smile on the girls again. "As a matter of fact, I was sitting here trying to decide which one of you I was going to try my best moves on. Being as how you are twins, I guess it doesn't matter, does it?"

They giggled, but Lee Bob said, "Now Dave, I know it's only the alcohol talking, but I don't hold with talking so forward to proper young ladies. Any more of that and I'm going to have to whomp you some."

"Are you kidding me? These young ladies are up for a good time, aren't you girls?"

"We're always up for fun," one of them said.

"Well I reckon we're going to have fun, all right, Lee Bob allowed. "But we're going to be gentlemen about it, if you know what's good for you."

The girls smiled at him, "How nice," Cathy said.

Lee Bob frowned as Dave muttered, "Yeah, how nice."

They sat out in the night air, ate pizzas and drank some wine they had ordered from room service, which the girls found much more to their taste. Lee Bob told them of the mountains, how the colors were so rich and vibrant when the sun came up over the horizon. He told them how it felt to walk in the early morning mist, trying for a trout in the cold running water. He told them about the animals and if you sat still and were patient, how they would come right up to you. The girls loved it.

Dave had long since passed out. The girls told Lee Bob of days on the beach and surfing and roller-skating along the beach front. He was fascinated. They traded stories until the early morning hours when he walked them back to their room and said good night. Then he came back and scooped Dave up like a rag doll to carry him back to his room with him.

He bedded Dave down on the couch and crawled into bed. It had been a very nice day.

Chapter 26

Dave woke up and sat upright. The movement caused him to put a hand to his head. "Where am I? My head feels big as a washtub and my mouth feels like a troop of Russian soldiers has been camped in it.""

Lee Bob said, "I fetched you in here and bedded you down last night. You didn't appear to be in any shape to travel, being as how you were out like a light."

"Thanks, I appreciate it. Did I have a good time?"

"You seemed to enjoy yourself a tolerable amount. You were a little rude to the girls, though. I was a mite peeved at you for it."

"Rude? Did I... I mean did we... well, was I with one of them?"

"You were with both of them up until you passed out on us. Then we kind of parked you while we visited a spell. They're right nice girls."

Suddenly Dave sat up. "What time is it?"

"Daybreak, I 'spect, maybe six a.m. Breakfast hasn't come yet."

"I wouldn't think so since I'm the one who's supposed to bring it. Mind if I take a shower?"

He must have just run through the shower because he was back in only minutes. "I got to go grab a clean uniform then make up something to tell the manager. I'll be back with your breakfast."

He ran out the door to return twenty minutes later with the

breakfast tray. He set it out, pocketed the tip and paused at the door. "Lee Bob, I know why you're here."

Lee Bob's eyebrows furrowed with suspicion, "How's that?"

"What you're here for is known in some places if a guy knows who to ask. I can be of help, for a price."

"Who knows?"

Dave turned from the door, hands held out defensively. "Nobody you need be concerned about. But I do know you're here for Junior. I know where he is and for a price I could save you a lot of time."

"How much?"

"Say $5,000."

He shook his head, "I ain't making all that much money on this deal."

"Well, how about $1,000 for his whereabouts? Anything else we can deal on."

"I'll go $500 and you quit nickel-and-diming me to death on these tips."

Dave held out his hand. "Done."

Lee Bob shook on the deal. "So, where is he?"

"The sheriff has him in protective custody up at the jail."

Lee Bob frowned. "You figure that's worth $500? I coulda found the same thing out down at the corner drug store."

"Maybe, with everybody knowing your business, but have you given any thought to how to get at him?"

Lee Bob walked over to the counter and poured himself another drink. He saw Dave visibly shudder at the thought and didn't bother to offer him one. "How would I get at him up there?"

"There could be a way, but it isn't necessary."

"Why not?"

Dave grinned. "Scuttlebutt has it the sheriff is taking him up to his cabin in the mountains for safekeeping."

Lee Bob relaxed. This was why he had been hired. "That's more like it!"

"You could get him as they bring him out of the jail."

"No, I want him up in the mountains where I know what I'm doing."

"You want me to keep an eye on him and let you know when they move him?"

Lee Bob tossed down the drink. "I thought you had to work."

"I can get a few days off. I'd do it for $100 bucks a day."

"Okay, if you'll throw in detailed instructions on how to get to the sheriff's cabin."

"Done."

Lee Bob looked worried. "The only thing I ain't too happy about is everybody and their dog knowing what I'm up to. I hadn't figured on that."

"Oh, it's not so many people." Dave paused. "Besides, talking about something and proving it, aren't the same thing at all... not by a long shot."

◊

It was late in the afternoon when Lee Bob opened the door to Dave. The bellman said, "You know they're on to you, don't you?"

"Who?"

"There's an unmarked sheriff's unit out there on stakeout now.

It has to be here to watch you."

"Ain't that a caution? Never had this much attention before 'ceptin' when I was making a run with a trunkload of shine."

"Well you had better be careful or all this attention will land you in jail." Dave plopped down into a chair. "Of course, you have an ace up your sleeve. They don't know about me."

"How about a little taste?" Lee Bob held out the bottle of Everclear.

Dave looked at it as if it were a live cobra. "No thanks. I don't have the constitution for it."

"Ya et yet?" Lee Bob made it one word.

"Beg your pardon?"

"Why, did you do something?"

"I mean, what did you say?"

Lee Bob sometimes felt like they needed a translator. "I was asking if you'd had supper."

"No."

"Let's order something, I hate to eat alone."

"You buying?"

Dave was beginning to get on his nerves. "Don't you ever think about anything but money?"

"Not very often."

"Well, then, yes, I'm buying."

He looked at the little man, he was probably right, I could be trying to hang on to some of this money, but the way I figure it, I'm going to be dirt poor again before I know it. The very best I could do would be to stall it off a little, and that wouldn't be any fun. It may be my only shot to enjoy it.

He looked at the little man. No point in telling him, there's no way he'd understand.

Dave was still on the subject. "Well, they got Jorgenson tucked away up at the jail, all right. They aren't making any effort to move him yet, but it's coming."

"What if they do it while you're here?"

"I got the place watched."

"You told somebody else?"

Dave looked offended, "No. Although I'd have trouble finding somebody in town to tell who doesn't already know. Actually, I've got a wino watching the place from across the street. All he knows is, if he'll call when they move anybody, I'll buy him a jug of wine." He added as an afterthought. "And in the meantime he isn't likely to attract any attention."

"You're very good at this."

"Given the fact of your existence being such a well-known fact, I must be better at it than you are. How about an introduction to your boss? I'll bet I could make a lot of money doing what you do."

"What I do, as you put it, ain't to be done in town. I was sent out here 'cause I know my way around up in them there mountains. I ain't supposed to try for him in town, but after he's fetched up to the cabin. They sent a big city feller after him before, and he didn't do so hot up there."

"I see. Well, have you decided yet what you intend to do about everybody knowing who you are?"

"I don't know. I got to think on it some."

Dave held out a cup. "Well, let me have a little taste of that high octane stuff. If I build my nerve up enough I may have a solution for you."

They had a meal poolside and soon Dave was showing the effects of the alcohol again while Lee Bob was again largely unaffected.

Lee Bob said, "You reckon we ought to go wake that guy up?"

"Who?"

"The big guy over there. He fell asleep by the pool. He's been there a long time."

"He's an Indian. He probably got his nose full of who-hit-john and passed out. The last thing I want to do is babysit a drunk."

"Well, all right," Lee Bob said. "But it don't seem neighborly."

"Don't worry, come closing time for the pool, the staff will get him back to his room."

"Staff? Back home a staff is a big stick. Dave, I don't mean to insult you or nothing, but I don't know what you're talking about half the time."

"You're a bit hard for me to understand as well. But now that I know what your specialty is, though, I don't underestimate you anymore."

"See there? I don't know what that means," Lee Bob admitted.

"Don't worry about it, it's only important that I do."

The little man was starting to slur his words and his eyes were hooded. If he was going to get anything out of him he had better hurry. "So have you worked up your courage yet?"

"Well, the solution to your problem is simple. You have to have an alibi for the time the deed is done. The way I see it, I can't go sneaking around in the woods like you can. But after you get all that stuff done, I could sit on Jorgenson until you had time to get somewhere and establish an alibi, and then snuff him for you."

"Why would you do that?"

"For half the money and for an introduction to the people who hired you and a recommendation based on doing the job. I said you were my ticket out of here."

"You're right, it could be the solution."

Dave raised his drink. "Here's to problems solved."

Lee Bob nodded and added, "To the Confederacy."

Dave rolled his eyes upwards.

◊

Little Bear walked into Buck's office to find him and Raul talking. Buck looked up and said, "Where you been?"

"I've been busy getting a handle on your boy."

"And?"

"He's about ready to make a move, and he's got help."

Buck raised an eyebrow, "So, who's helping him?"

Little Bear dropped heavily into a chair. "That meatball Dave Walovich out at the motel. You know, the one who thinks he's just a little smarter than everybody else in the known world?"

"Yeah, I always figured he was going to go a little too far milking the tourists, and we'd get to put him up in our little steel motel for a while."

Raul said, "Oh, yeah, I do think it would do him good to hustle bags here for a while."

Buck looked intently at his friend, "So, how does Walovich fit into this?"

"He sees this guy as his ticket to the big time," Little Bear said. "He plans to help Courtland establish an alibi since we know who Courtland is."

"Why, the only way he could do that is... "

"Exactly, he'd have to pull the trigger. He can't try to cut Courtland out, though. He needs him to get paid since he doesn't have the connections himself."

"You're gonna need help for sure now."

"Yes, I may need an extra pair of eyes with me."

"So we'll go back to what I originally suggested."

"Buck, I really don't want to hurt your feelings, but you're a bull in a china shop out in the woods. You'd get me killed, no offense intended."

"None taken. I know I haven't had any offers to dance ballet lately. So what do you suggest?"

"How about me?" Raul asked.

"That would be like trying to hide an eighteen wheeler," Little Bear told the big deputy. "Actually, before it was over last time, Wayne was starting to get around pretty good."

"I don't like it. I'd get skinned if you got him shot."

"Don't worry, he won't get anywhere near them. All I need him for is to keep an eye on that weasel Walovich if they split up. Wayne's more than a match for him now that I've been working with him, and I won't let him get anywhere near Courtland."

"Well, all right, but it makes me very uncomfortable."

"He'll do fine."

"How did you come up with all of this information?"

"Laid right under their noses on a lounge chair. They thought I was a drunk."

Chapter 27

Dave came to Lee Bob's door early in the morning. Lee Bob said, "Morning, Dave. Early for you, ain't it?"

"My wino called. They're loading Jorgenson into a patrol car."

"I'm ready. All my mountain gear is in the trunk of the car."

"Let's go. We can pick up on them over at the intersection."

They parked in an abandoned service station and waited until the patrol car came by, driven by a big Mexican. The sheriff and Jorgenson were clearly visible in the rear of the car.

Lee Bob pulled out a discreet distance behind them, but in less than half a mile, he saw flashing lights in the rear view mirror.

"Huh-oh," Lee Bob said.

"Don't worry about it." Dave slipped on sunglasses and leaned back against the door pretending to be asleep. "They're only trying to get you off his tail. We know where they're going."

Lee Bob watched the officer stroll to the window. "Your license, and registration sir," the officer said, before explaining that the car had a tail light out. He let them go with a warning.

◊

Of course they had a tail light out. Little Bear had seen to it the night before.

During the short interval, Raul had stopped, Buck and Junior had gotten out and Little Bear and Wayne had gotten in. Then Raul headed out again at a leisurely rate of speed. Buck and Junior waited with Little Bear's old truck until they saw the pursuers pass, intent on catching up.

◊

As soon as they got the patrol car back in sight, Lee Bob eased up on the gas. "Looks like they didn't jerk us around long enough, doesn't it?"

Dave nodded. "Looks like it."

When the patrol car turned into the ranch, Lee Bob and Dave pulled off out of sight. Soon the patrol car came back to the entrance and stayed there.

It wasn't long before Lee Bob saw two riders and a couple of pack animals going up over the ridge. "There they go."

After the patrol unit drove off toward town, they got their gear from the trunk and headed after them avoiding being spotted by anyone at the ranch headquarters.

◊

"So, what's our game plan?" Wayne asked.

"It will not take our friend long to find the cabin. We do not wish him to find us there, so we will use it for bait instead."

"Are you going to do the snake and the animal things again?"

"We may try a thing or two just to see what we are up against. In the meantime, we must situate ourselves where we can keep an eye on them. The advantage will be ours as they will be expecting to initiate contact at the cabin."

"So we don't go to the cabin?"

"I don't. You do."

Wayne gave him a puzzled look as the Indian stepped down and pulled a small pack off his horse. "I need you to take all the horses to the cabin. Build a fire and stay there long enough to get a couple of real good sized logs going in the fireplace. You should be able to get it done in twenty or thirty minutes. When the fire is satisfactory, take two of the horses back up over the hill behind the cabin and circle around to wait for me over at the windmill. Leave plenty of food out for the pack horses you will be leaving. You do remember the place where the windmill is, don't you?"

"Yes."

"Be sure you leave the stable door closed, so they can't tell from a distance all the horses aren't in there."

"No problem. What will you be doing?"

"Watching. I can't get out ahead of this guy the way I did the other one. I'll have to watch for any opportunities and then try to exploit them."

◊

"This thing weighs a ton," Dave complained.

What a weenie, Lee Bob already regretted bringing the man. "You'll get used to it."

"I hope I don't have to lug it around long enough to get used to it."

"This will take a couple of days at best."

Dave looked astonished. "You mean we're going to sleep out here?"

"What did you think you're carrying that bedroll for?"

188

"Is that what that is?"

Give me a break. "That's what it is. My memory ain't all that good, but wasn't it your idea for you to come along?"

"Yeah... yeah... don't rub it in."

"You starting to crawfish on me?" Lee Bob asked.

"Crawfish? What does that mean?"

"It means are you backing out?"

"No, it's going to be worth it." He hitched the pack up higher on his shoulder and Lee Bob heard him mumble, "At least it had better be worth it."

Across the little meadow, they came to the stream. Lee Bob examined it. "Those directions you got weren't very good, but unless they have a well, the cabin pretty much has to be somewhere up this stream. We'll follow it and see what we find."

They cut across to intersect the point where Lee Bob had seen the horses going over the crest of the hill and picked up their tracks. "Here they are. It'll be easy to follow these to the cabin."

It took several hours before they reached the spot where they could see the little cabin across the valley, smoke pouring lazily from its chimney.

"There it is," Lee Bob said.

"Okay, let's go get them."

"Oh, no, a man could really get hurt running into a cave after a varmint. Once you run something to ground, you had better take the time to find out exactly what you're up against before you go off half-cocked."

"Is that supposed to make some kind of sense?"

Lee Bob shook his head. "It means we'll watch the place for a spell before we do something stupid."

"Looks to me like we could jump in there, get it done, and not have to sleep out in the woods like a bear or tiger, or something."

"Not a good idea. We'll drop back over the ridge where they won't see our fire. We'll fix a little something to eat."

Dave continued to grumble, but Lee Bob just ignored him.

◊

They moved over in a small draw where Lee Bob made a nearly smokeless fire, impressing Little Bear, who watched from the hill. What little smoke the dry wood gave off dissipated in the trees on the slope above. When they started to fry some bacon and pan bread, Little Bear slipped by the cabin to put wood on the fire, then went to meet Wayne.

He found Wayne sitting, eating some Vienna sausages, with cheese and crackers. It sounded like a good idea, so Little Bear joined him. He felt a little guilty that he wasn't proving he could hide a fire as well as Courtland, but it was a fleeting thought.

Little Bear speared a sausage and cut off a piece of cheese. Talking around the food in his mouth, he said, "We'll make a cold camp in the brush over on the other side of the windmill. There's no reason for them to come over there."

"Cold camp?"

"No fire."

"Okay, what do you need from me?"

Little Bear pulled out another can of the little sausages. "Nothing yet. Just be here. I can't tell you how important it is for you to stay far away from this man. He is part of the mountains. He wears them like a shirt. He doesn't even have to see you. If you are near, he can feel you."

"I understand."

"I'm serious, you have to realize you must do nothing without my specific instructions."

"I get it."

The second can disappeared as fast as the first one had. "Very well. I must get back and watch them. At some point, the coyote will sleep and will set the rabbit to watch. When he sleeps, I will sleep, and you must watch the rabbit for me."

"You're talking about Walovich?"

"Yes. So you might get a little sleep yourself if you can."

"I'll be right here when you need me."

◊

After they ate, Lee Bob told Dave he should get some sleep so he could stand a watch later. Dave rolled up in a blanket and complied immediately..

Lee Bob headed off to the cabin, where he sat motionlessly watching. Then he circled the cabin. The fire had burned down, but in the dim glow, he could see forms on the two beds..

Lee Bob was tempted to slip in and take them, but in spite of their apparently unprepared state, he knew it would be foolish. They might have an alarm or a trap, or there might be someone else around.

"Best to be sure," he whispered to the night as he finished his circle. He was surprised to find only two horses in the stable. "Guess they turned the pack horses loose to return to the ranch."

He returned to his vantage point and resumed his watch.

◊

Little Bear watched the search, then turned his attention to the camp. He had no trouble slipping through the camp without waking Dave. As he'd done before, he slipped a snake into Lee Bob's bedroll. This time he used a rattlesnake. As before, the snake took to the residual body warmth and settled in for the duration.

◊

Lee Bob returned to camp a little after two in the morning and woke Dave. He took off his boots, then checked his bedroll for any unwanted visitors before climbing in. Finding one, he flipped the covers over the snake's head, grabbed it by the tail, and popped it like a bullwhip, snapping the head off.

"Quite a juicy one," he began to skin it.

Dave's eyes were huge. "Why are you skinning that thing?"

"To roast it, of course. Snake is delicious."

Dave shuddered.

Lee Bob only slept a few hours, but it was enough. He awoke, stretched, and laced his boots to go relieve Dave. The fool was probably asleep.

As he was securing the laces, he noticed a curious scuff mark. He puzzled over it, then started looking further. As he passed the fire, he got a cup of coffee and a big tube of roasted snake. Holding it like an ice cream bar, he found a couple of more scuff marks, bent grass and a broken twig or two.

He slipped up next to Dave, who surprised him by being

awake. "Any sign of movement?" he asked.

"No."

"Curious, the sun's up, and no smoke from the chimney."

"Lee Bob, what are you eating?"

"The roast snake. It's great." He pulled another piece from his pocket. "Want some?"

"I'd rather eat toxic waste."

Lee Bob shrugged and went back to watching the cabin. "I think we had a visitor at the camp last night."

"A visitor?"

"Yes, I'd say while you were asleep. If I'd been there I'd have heard him."

"How can you be so sure?"

"He was wearing very soft soles, probably moccasins, but there were marks."

"Whoever it was could have fixed my wagon."

"Reckon so. I'm not sure why he didn't. I've been thinking on it some."

Lee Bob suddenly stood up. Dave hissed, "They'll see you."

"I don't think so. I 'spect if anybody was here, he'd have built a breakfast fire, or fed the stock long before this. Somebody is playing games with us."

They walked into the cabin. Lee Bob threw back the covers to show the pillows and blankets forming the mounds. The ashes in the fireplace were barely warm. The water bucket was bone dry, and the dust on the table testified no one had been there any longer than it took to build up the fire.

"So that's why there were only two horses... "

"What does this mean?" Dave asked.

"If you're going to set a snare, you've got to put out bait. Looks like they knew we were coming. This cabin is bait."

"Bait for what? What kind of trap?"

"I don't know. One thing for sure, whoever is out there is watching us, and they're watching us right now."

◊

Little Bear watched them go in the cabin, knowing he should have slipped in the back way and built a breakfast fire because this fellow had discovered the ruse far too quickly. He wasn't going to be easy to deal with, but it was as he had expected.

He continued to watch as the pair went back to their camp, built up the fire and began fixing something to eat. Little Bear slipped back over to his own camp.

◊

Lee Bob never saw his observer, not coming or going, but he _felt_ when he was no longer there. He told Dave he was going to go take a look around.

"You just now started cooking."

"You take it over."

"I can't cook."

"You only have to watch it until it looks done, then take it off and eat it." When Dave looked unconvinced, he chuckled, said, "Or get you some snake and eat it."

Dave squatted and started stirring the bacon around. Lee Bob circled the camp until he found the man's tracks. The person watching had been good. Just not good enough.

Lee Bob followed the trail, working it out a piece at a time. Half way through the valley he smelled, but didn't see smoke. He crouched down to scan the area until he saw some faint traces in the thicket on the other side of the windmill. He kept the windmill between him and the smoke as he carefully closed the gap.

Two men sat eating. He studied them. The big man had obviously made the tracks. Seeing the man's size, Lee Bob was very impressed by how little he had found. The smaller man did not seem to be as much at home in the camp. His movements weren't those of a woodsman. Yes, the big man was his adversary. He returned his attention to him. Suddenly, the man's head jerked up.

Lee Bob knew he'd let the fellow feel his eyes by studying him for too long. He pulled his rifle to his shoulder and sighted.

◊

"What's the matter?" Wayne asked.

"I don't know, something... "

Suddenly, Little Bear's coffee cup spun out of his hand. A split second later, the sound of a shot followed it, but Little Bear was already on his way to the ground. Following his lead, Wayne dived for the log he had been sitting on, feeling a tug at his leg as another shot sounded. A third shot, and the coffee pot careened into the brush. Then all was quiet.

"I'm hit," Wayne said, hysteria in his voice. "I can feel the blood."

Little Bear slipped to his side. "What you feel is only my

coffee. He shot the heel off your boot, though."

"Guess I was moving too fast. Good thing he wasn't a better shot."

"He hit everything he shot at, and he hit only the heel of your boot with you flying through the air. From the lag in the sound of the shot, he did it from a couple of hundred yards away. I'd say over by the windmill."

"Is he still there?"

"My guess would be no, but it would be foolish to not check. Stay under cover."

The big Indian melted into the brush. It took him only a few minutes to insure the man was gone and to discover his tracks.

"Pack up."

"We're leaving?"

"You are."

"I'm not leaving you here by yourself. I'm not afraid."

"I don't question your courage, my friend, but our adversary has taken the initiative. I must have a counter move. I want you to leave, and I want you to go by the cabin and take all the horses. I want him to think we've left. I'll ride with you as far as the rock shelf by the creek and dismount there."

"When do I come back?"

"You don't. It would be suicide to come back into this situation blind without knowing where all the players are."

"All right, but I don't like it."

Little Bear smiled to himself. It was true the outgoing trail might give him a momentary edge, but his real purpose was to remove Wayne from danger. He was pleased he could help him save face, though. Saving face was important.

◊

"I think I scared them off." Lee Bob told his companion.

"Really?"

"I watched them ride away and trailed them until they turned into the canyon."

"Jorgenson wasn't with them?"

"No, we'll give the area a good search to make sure they aren't camping out, then we'll go back and start over."

Dave looked ecstatic. "We can't go back too soon for me."

"You know, it's funny."

"What is?"

He knew what he saw, but it was bothering him. "I wouldn't have figured on the big Indian quitting this easily. It doesn't feel right."

"It wouldn't take me long if somebody was shooting at me."

"No, I'm sure it wouldn't, but I figured the Indian to be a different breed of cat." Lee Bob got a cup of coffee and looked into it as if it contained the answer to his questions. "Maybe he was only removing the other man from danger."

He looked at Dave and suddenly realized the man was no longer any help. In fact, he had become a liability. In the same instant, he knew the Indian would be back.

Chapter 28

Lee Bob and Dave packed their gear. "You know you don't know nothin' about searching the woods for somebody," Lee Bob said. "You'll do more good going back and trying to get a lead on Jorgenson back there."

"Yeah, I'll buy that. Back there we're playing *my* game." He looked concerned. "You aren't coming?"

"No. I have to be sure they aren't up here somewhere first."

"But I don't have a clue how to get out of here. I don't even know which direction it is." Dave's tone bordered on whining.

"Don't worry, all you have to do is follow the stream. It'll take you right to the car."

Dave didn't seem convinced. "What if I run into them?"

"You won't. I figure the young guy is hot-footing it to town to warn them, and I plan to keep the Indian occupied."

◊

Without telling Little Bear what he planned, Wayne left a little present as he passed the men's car. Four flat tires would slow either of the men down because he'd have to walk to the ranch or to town for help.

Wayne saw to it that the hands knew to take either or both of the men to town to find help instead of helping directly This would occupy them for the better part of the day in trying to resolve the problem.

Once he was back in town, Wayne brought Buck up to date. Buck's reaction was predictable. "Why didn't he come back with you if they were on to you? Crazy Indian."

"I think it's a matter of pride."

"Sure it's a matter of pride, but pride doesn't do you much good when you're dead." He paced up and down his office a couple of times, then he threw up his hands. "Well, there's nothing we can do now. Whatever is going to happen will happen before we could get back up there. Little Bear warned us, which is what he intended to do."

He put his hand on the boy's shoulder. "I'll tell you this, between the two of you, you've bought us the time to prepare."

Junior agreed. "I think I ought to get out of here and give the feds a call. I don't want to put you guys in danger."

"How many times do we have to go through this, Junior? There's no place safer than the jail. Here you know who's after you and where they are. Sure, there's danger here, but you gotta see your odds are still much better than anywhere else."

"I guess so."

Buck looked at Raul. "I want extra officers in here, and I want them briefed and alert."

"You got it."

◊

Little Bear scanned the countryside. He figured Lee Bob was doing the same thing, looking for him. This was the first time he'd ever hunted something that hunted him back, and he relished the challenge.

Where to start? The only place he could think of was their camp, but it would be tough to figure out which trail out was freshest. Besides, he'd really be vulnerable while he scouted there.

Where would this Lee Bob fellow choose to start?

Suddenly, he knew. The other man would have to begin at the last place he knew Little Bear had been, which was be the trail out of the canyon. He'd have to figure out where Little Bear had dismounted and pick the trail up from there. Little Bear didn't waste a single minute thinking he had fooled the man, or that Lee Bob imagined him gone from the mountain.

He would wait for the man to pick up his trail. "All right, so where do I lead him?" he said aloud as he looked around.

A spot just after he crossed a stream provided a trail floor lined with leaves. He rigged a log deadfall snare, hiding the trip rope and the snare under the leaves. He carefully restored the leaves to a natural look.

The Indian knew it wouldn't work if the other man were paying attention, because there was simply no way to get all the leaves dry side up in the time available. He needed to get the man's attention focused on up the trail.

A few yards later, he hastily rigged a bent tree snare, hiding the rope well. He figured the bent tree would catch the eye of an experienced woodsman like a signal light, so he went on up the ridge to watch.

He saw when Lee Bob found the trail where it came off the rock shelf, trailing Little Bear to the stream and across, immediately spotting the bent tree. He smiled and said loudly, knowing his adversary was within the sound of his voice, "I'm disappointed. You're gonna have to do a lot better than this if you figure to catch this old... *yeow!*"

The rest of his sentence was lost the snare swept him up into the air. He could hear the deadfall crashing off to the side as it provided the impetus that jerked him up.

Little Bear started forward to get to him before he recovered, but found that the other man had a large knife out even as he shot up in the snare. As his weight descended, he sliced through the rope and hit the ground rolling.

The speed of the man's reaction startled Little Bear, forcing him into the brush. His quarry lay perfectly still as if he had heard Little Bear's approach.

◊

His adversary was close, deadly close. He had heard him coming in and Lee Bob knew if it had taken him any longer to get out of the trap, the game would have been over.

Game? Yes, I gotta admit it, I'm enjoying this. A deadly game, true, but still I ain't had this much fun in years. His eyes continued to slowly scan, probing for any sign, any movement. A deadly game? Is that true? Does this guy intend to kill me? There was no way to know, but he didn't intend to give him the chance.

Moving deathly slow, he began to break it off, backing away without a sound, trying to leave as little sign of his passing as possible. A confrontation here offered no advantage to either, and he was sure his adversary knew it as well as he did.

◊

Little Bear retreated to a high cliff he knew. It had a small depression, less than a cave, but deep enough to hide a fire. The rock shelf below hid tracks very well, but the loose shale scattered about would announce anyone moving in. The cliff was high enough his place could not be reached from the top. It was very secure. Here he could get the rest he needed. He was sure this Lee Bob character would be doing the same.

After a couple hours sleep he picked up Lee Bob's trail and followed it for a couple of miles deep into the woods. He found the camp, a fire and saw a form rolled up in a blanket by the fire. But something wasn't right and Little Bear used his glasses slowly panning the area. Then something moved.

Lee Bob had been sleeping up in a fork of a tree. Now he was coming down and Little Bear watched with interest as the man began work on a deadfall snare of his own. This guy is a pro! If I hadn't seen him working on it, I might have blundered right into it.

He could tell the man was inspecting his work, looking for any telltale sign. Then he apparently saw something and stepped inside carefully to correct it. It was what Little Bear had been hoping for. As the man carefully placed his foot to reach for whatever he wanted to fix, Little Bear sighted his rifle on the stake holding the trip rope secure and gently squeezed the trigger.

Little Bear could see the man's eyes go wide as the shot sounded and the snare jerked tight on his foot. Little Bear heard, "NOT AGAIN!" the last word trailing off at the end, as the man sailed up in the air.

This time Little Bear knew better than to rush in and immediately withdrew as he saw Lee Bob slicing the rope, rolling as he landed just as he had done before.

◊

When he was sure he was alone, Lee Bob considered what had happened. He now realized the big Indian wasn't trying to kill him because he could have shot him as easily as he had shot that trip rope. Still, catching a man in his own trap was pretty insulting.

◊

Little Bear returned to the cliff for a few hours' sleep and a bite of breakfast. He pondered the man's next move. He felt sure he would move his camp? Would he set another trap? Almost certainly. A few quick bites and he rolled up in his blankets.

A couple of hours later he heard the sound of shale rattling. He looked over the edge to see Lee Bob trying to track him over the rock ledge. He was impressed the man had followed the tracks to the ledge after he had swept tracks, backtracked and used a variety of other tricks to mask the trail.

He knew what the man was finding below, however. He would find some scuff marks, but they would give him no clue as to direction. Then he saw the man stop to search the cliff with his eyes, seeing nothing.

Little Bear watched him continue to search until he finally found the place where Little Bear had left the shelf earlier. He began to follow the tracks, tracks that would lead the man back to his own camp. Little Bear settled back down to finish his nap.

◊

"Now isn't this interesting," Lee Bob said as he realized he was coming back to his former camp again. "Looks like he up and disappeared."

He gathered his gear, then moved out to find a new camp. He wondered what his next move would be. "Guess I could go back over the trail and see if I can find where he got off of it." He thought on it a minute, then shook his head. "No, if he was on the side when I went by, then he probably had me under his gun the whole time. If I go pushing him too far, he might decide to plug me after all."

He sat and ate some jerky as he thought over the problem. Finally, he made up his mind. Okay, to do anything with this guy I'm gonna have to have some bait, and the best bait out here is *me*.

Moving away from Little Bear's trail, Lee Bob headed further upstream, covering his trail as he went. This time, he took care not to get the job done completely. He wanted to be followed, but didn't want it to look like he was inviting it.

Finally, he found what he was looking for, an area where the stream went through a fairly narrow cut. To Lee Bob this meant three things: first, his pursuer would have to pass on the trail; second, he would be suspicious of the natural ambush spot with his attention focused ahead; finally, he would have to proceed very slowly.

He decided to use the bent-tree trick the Indian had used on him to distract him away from the real trap. This time, however, the tree would be bent sideways around a big tree stump, hidden behind a large bush. When released, it would sweep the trail and would do it with a lot of force. There would be no snare for the man to see and no trip wire to give it away. Lee Bob would trigger it himself.

It would be a long chance, of course, but Lee Bob counted on the Indian being very suspicious of the possible ambush up ahead. He ran the trip wire where he could trigger it from the tree above the trail, then he climbed up the tree to wait.

Waiting took patience, which Lee Bob had learned in the woods. The Indian approached silently, stopping periodically to study tracks. For a large man he was incredibly agile.

A normal person seldom looks up, but Lee Bob knew he couldn't count on this from someone at home in the woods. No, the threat of the narrow passage had to occupy the man's attention, or he'd be toast.

The man behaved just as Lee Bob hoped, sweeping the path with his gaze and ducking to peer through the narrow opening. As Indian slid very slowly beneath him, Lee Bob triggered the trip rope.

The tree came out of the brush with a *whoosh,* catching the Indian squarely in the center of his generous belly. All the air left him in an, *"Uhhhh!"* nearly as loud as the swish made by the tree.

Lee Bob jumped down quickly to tie the hands and feet of the big Indian. It took several minutes for the Indian to regain his senses, during which time Lee Bob shaved chunks of jerky off a big piece with his knife and shoved them in his mouth. He noticed the Indian looking at him. "You going to be okay?"

"I think I'm going to have some very sore ribs, maybe even some broken ones, if I live to worry about them, that is."

"Oh, I wouldn't think they were life-threatening," Lee Bob

said, smiling.

"I wasn't thinking in terms of my ribs."

Lee Bob hadn't tied him, but had taken his gun and held his own weapon in his lap. "Oh, you mean me. I ain't gonna hurt you none. There ain't enough genuine mountain men left in this old world but what we can afford to lose one."

"I wouldn't expect your type to think that way."

"My type? What is it you figure you know about my type?"

"I know you're a killer."

"Now, there you go." Lee Bob waved the knife his way, disgusted. "I ain't no killer. Never killed nobody in my whole life."

"But you're about to."

"We all have to do things we don't want to do."

"That's a lot to have to live with."

The big man's words nagged at him. "You let me worry about that. I'm gonna take your horse and your moccasins. That ought to slow you down enough to give me all the lead time I need."

Chapter 29

Dave was in Lee Bob's room when he returned. "I got your information for you."

"Okay, what'd you find out?"

"I already knew that during the day the courthouse is generally a beehive of activity, even more if there are any trials in progress. But after five things settle down to a couple of dozen. A lot of them would be cops though."

"Sounds like a small army to me."

"It would be, but in the wee hours of the morning it'd be different. There'd be a jailer upstairs, a night dispatcher and three patrol officers that would be out in the field most of the time."

"Two of them? And one only a dispatcher? I could work with that."

"You could, and you'd be walking right into their trap."

"Trap?"

Dave puffed up like a toad, "You be so lost without me. The Sheriff is figuring on you making a try. The day shift today was a skeleton crew. He's got a half dozen officers in that building at night and they aren't parking in the parking lot. Like I say, it's a trap."

"We could set fire to the place and force them out."

Dave shook his head, "No, they'd only secure the outside and it'd bring everybody in town running. He'd probably get swallowed up in the crowd, but even if he didn't, if we got him we'd have a devil of a time getting away."

"Yeah, I guess you're right."

"What we need is a diversion. We need something to pull those extra officers away from the building."

Lee Bob was skeptical. "When they're sitting on a prisoner they know somebody is after? You think they'd do that?"

Dave smiled an evil grin. "There's one thing, one thing no cop can resist."

"What's that?"

"The sound of a cop in trouble. When the radio yells, "Officer needs assistance!" every cop comes running, no matter what they're doing. I don't think they'd even stop to think."

Just when he started thinking Dave didn't have the sense to pour water out of a boot with the directions written on the heel the little man would surprise him. "That's it, then. How do we do it?"

"There's a bunch of juvenile delinquents who hang out over at the east side pool hall. Give me a little money and I can have them jumping through hoops to help."

"All right, but we have to move fast, I have a little lead time but not that much."

"We'll do it tonight."

◊

"What am I missing, Raul?"

"Sounds to me like you've got it covered."

"I hope so," Buck said. "I'm going to go to the house here in a few minutes to get a little sleep, then I'll be back down here to be on hand in the early hours."

"You think they'll try it then?"

Buck went over to retrieve his hat from the hat rack. "I do, and if they make a try, that when it has to be done."

"What if they bring more help in?"

Buck put the hat on and walked to the door. "I'm sure we would have spotted them if there were new people in town, but I can't imagine them trying it alone either. Come to think of it, I can't imagine Dave in this sort of thing in any manner. I always thought he was all talk and no show."

"It doesn't look to me like they have any chance at all."

"Looks like it to me, too," Buck said. "Maybe they'll wake up to that fact and pack it in."

"Maybe they will, but I wouldn't count on it. Well, you better go get some sleep."

"Yeah, I guess so. If I can."

◊

There were three units in the field to respond when the call came in. Someone had triggered the alarm at the First National Bank. All three units headed there, lights flashing and sirens blaring. The shift supervisor left the sheriff's office to meet them.

The dispatcher decided not to wake Buck up until an emergency was confirmed. When a train came through town, it often set off alarms, as did some of the high, West Texas winds.

The units arrived on the scene, but saw nothing except a broken window in a back door. They couldn't tell if entry had been made. They were about to have dispatch call Buck when suddenly little blossoms of orange bloomed on the tops of several neighboring buildings, and hot little hornets filled the air. Nasty whines resounded as the bullets ricocheted off the building and sidewalk. Sounds like popcorn popping reached their ears.

They dove behind the units and put the dreaded call on the air: "*Officer needs assistance, shots fired!* As one man, the officers remaining in the office sprinted for their cars.

He picked up the phone on the second ring. "This is Buck."

The voice was very excited. "Sheriff, we have units under fire over at the bank. There seems to be a large group of unknown assailants."

Buck sat up and reached for his pants. "Back 'em up, call for help from other agencies, but keep two or three officers at the jail. I'm on my way."

"Everybody is gone already."

"*What*? Get up now and go lock all the doors, then re-call at least four officers, no matter what's going on. I'll be there in three minutes... Move!

He shaved several seconds off the three minutes by still having his house shoes and pajama top on. Skidding into the parking lot, he jumped out and sprinted for the door. It wasn't locked as he had ordered. Running in he looked over at the switchboard, but the dispatcher wasn't there.

"*Crap!*" he yelled as he ran to get a gun from the gun case. As he opened the case, he felt the cold steel of a shotgun press into his neck.

"If you're thinking about being a hero and trying to spin around and get this gun, my finger is a lot faster."

Buck raised his hands. "Where are my people?"

"The nice lady who came to lock the door went to sleep when I tapped her with Dave's lead sap," Lee Bob said. "She's tied up in your office."

"My men will be back soon."

"I reckon that's true enough, so we'd better hurry. 'Course, I'd say they're still ducking bullets right now."

"Who's doing the shooting?"

"You start walking, I'll tell you on the way." They started up the stairs to the jail. "It's some of your local little darlings."

"Kids?"

"Sure thing. They'll make it hot for your boys for a while, and then they'll give up. Being as how they're only kids, nobody will be able to do much of anything to them." He stopped and yelled, "Hello, the jail."

"Who is that?" the jailer asked.

"Open up, I got the sheriff, and I got a gun screwed into his ear."

"Buck, you out there?"

"Yes, but don't you be opening up the door."

"You listen to him, and you're gonna have one dead sheriff on your hands, then I'll simply set fire to the place and shoot you as you come out. If you play this smart, nobody has to get hurt."

The jailer stayed out of sight but said, "Nobody?"

"Well, Jorgenson is going to have to come with me, but the rest of you will be all right."

"Don't listen to him, Jim," Buck shouted. The yell brought a shotgun butt into his stomach.

"What was that? Buck, are you all right?"

"The sheriff is a little winded right now. You gonna open the door, or are we going to do this the hard way?"

The door opened, and Lee Bob had all three of them under his gun.

"Mr. Jorgenson, you're gonna need to step out here."

"No, I don't think so. I think I'll require you to shoot me right here."

"Guess I can do it if I have to, but then I gotta shoot them, too to eliminate the witnesses. If you come with me, then I can just lock them fellows up."

"All right, I'll come."

Buck stepped between them and turned to face the man, his hands still held in the air. "Son, you don't look like the kind of man who'd do this."

"Looks can deceive you, sure 'nuff. We all do what we have to do."

"Yes, and I know what I have to do." Buck turned and told the jailer to go back into the cell block and lock himself in. The man didn't move. "It's an order!" he barked.

The jailer walked off, and Buck turned back to the man.

"You'd best be getting back there with him, Sheriff."

"No. I'm like Junior. I think I'll require you to shoot me right here."

"Buck, don't be a fool," Junior said.

"I'd listen to your friend. I don't relish shooting no cop, but I wouldn't advise you to call my hand on it."

"Son, you ever heard of the ten commandments? 'Thou shalt not kill' is a big rock to have to climb over to get into Heaven."

"Aw, I figure I already blown my ticket there."

"How? Moonshining? Out this way, we don't think that's much of a big deal. The way I see it, you haven't done anything to cancel your ticket yet, but you sure enough have got your foot in the door. What are you doing this for? Money? Fame? You know none of that will stand up against throwing away life in the hereafter."

"You don't talk like no sheriff. You sound more like a preacher."

"Funny you should say that."

They stood there for what seemed like hours, though it wasn't more than a minute or so. Then the muzzle of the gun lowered very slightly, but came right back on line.

"I reckon you're right, Sheriff. I ain't no killer."

"I didn't think you were, son. How about you give me the shotgun?"

"No, I don't think I can. Don't press your luck, Sheriff. I'm offering to back out of here. Don't force me to shoot you after all, cause if I start, then I gotta go ahead and do the job."

"You ought to give yourself up, son. I'd do all I could for you. I could probably get you into the Witness Protection Program."

"I reckon you really believe it, Sheriff, but going back to jail without doing what they sent me to do would be a death sentence, and I see how good the Witness Protection Program is doing for Mr. Jorgenson here." He got a funny sort of smile on his face. "I got a better Witness Protection Program. If they want to come after me up in the hills, they'll find out what government men have found for years when they tried to run somebody down up there.

There's millions of places to hide, and everybody is kin to me. They don't take kindly to strangers, neither."

"That sounds like witness protection to me. Little Bear said you were a good man."

"He the Indian?"

"Yes, he called on the radio to warn us you were coming."

"He's a good man, too."

"I see my units are coming back. Since you're probably going down these back stairs, I guess you'll miss them."

"Why are you helping me?"

"I'm not helping. I was only guessing what you were going to do."

"Well, you sure enough called it." Lee Bob disappeared through the door.

Buck went back to let the jailer out of the cell, then he and Junior went downstairs to walk right into a zoo. Buck found Raul. "Whatcha got?"

"A bunch of babies who think they're the Al Capone mob. Somebody bought them guns and put them up on the roof to shoot at us when we showed up."

Buck let out a long, ragged sigh. "Yeah, and I can guess who and why. Somebody take Mrs. Wilson to the emergency room to get her head looked at. Now, let's get this sorted out."

Chapter 30

By midmorning, Buck and his crew had restored order. Mrs. Wilson was all right, the kids found themselves at the regional juvenile detention center, and all-points bulletins were issued on Lee Bob and Dave. Then Buck looked up to see Jim Minor coming in with Barney.

"Morning, Barney. Morning Jim." Buck wanted to ask Jim how he thought his campaign was going, but thought it might be in bad taste. Jim gave him a clue anyway.

"Morning, Buck. Good to have you working on my campaign for me."

"What would make you think I'm doing that?"

"All that foolishness last night has to work in my favor. Your letting the bank get robbed for example. I expect it's going to look real careless to the voters."

"The bank wasn't robbed. It was simply a case of vandalism. A window was broken, but no entry was made. My officers got on it too fast." Barney wasn't saying anything, but was taking notes.

"How about a shoot-out downtown? The voters deserve to feel more secure in their homes."

"It was only a bunch of kids. We rounded them up and have them over at juvenile detention. As a matter of fact, they're likely to be over there for a long time, which is bound to make a big difference in the vandalism and petty thefts around town. I'll bet the voters will feel more secure when these punks aren't out there, trying to steal anything not tied down."

"Got an answer for everything, don't you?" Minor sneered. "Let's see you explain away the escaped prisoner."

"There is no escaped prisoner. Junior Jorgenson was in jail on protective custody. We have reason to believe the danger has passed, so he checked himself out."

"You expect me to buy that when you have an all-points bulletin out on two men?"

"Jim, if you don't mind a little tip on how to run a campaign for Sheriff, you really ought to check out your facts before you go spouting off in front of the media. We have an APB out on these guys because we suspect them of being a threat to Junior. We suspect Dave of being behind the misbehavior of these kids."

"Well... well... . Barney, aren't you going to ask any questions?"

"Sounds like you got them asked. I'd say the story so far is, 'Sheriff's candidate accuses sheriff of mishandling job.' Facts show in one night the sheriff foiled a bank robbery, rounded up a gang of juvenile delinquents, scared off assailants who were threatening a man's life, and is well on his way to apprehending a man responsible for contributing to the delinquency of a minor. I want to thank you, Jim. Buck is so quiet and unassuming, I might not have gotten this story without your help."

"You wouldn't print it like that! It's a white-wash job."

"Not the way I see it.

Minor snorted and stomped off.

"Thanks, Barney."

"Looks like the story isn't ready to go to bed yet, though. It looks like another piece is walking in now."

Buck turned to see a DPS trooper coming in the door with Dave in handcuffs.

"Well, Dave, I knew we'd get you to check into *our* hotel one of these days."

Dave blustered, "Would you tell this storm trooper there's a mistake being made here?"

"There sure is, Dave, only you're the one who made it."

"I haven't done anything."

"We know you were involved in a thwarted attempt on Junior Jorgenson's life, but we can't prove it."

Dave put a big smile on his face.

"However, we have ample testimony from all of those misguided young people to charge you with attempted robbery of the First National Bank, accessory to attempted murder of a police officer, and contributing to the delinquency of a minor. There will be several counts filed on each of the latter two charges."

The smile disappeared. "Now wait, I... "

Buck held up his hand. "I'd advise you to not say anything until you have a lawyer."

"Where's Lee Bob?"

Buck turned back to him, "Lee Bob who?"

"Lee Bob Courtland, that's who."

"We have some unsubstantiated information a person by that name may have assisted you in some of your nefarious activities."

"Assisted *me*! I did some stuff for *him*!" Dave's voice went up almost a full octave. "How about we cut a little deal? I can roll over on him, if you'll drop the charges against me."

Buck held out one hand, palm up. "Let me get this straight. You want me to drop the charges against a man facing multiple counts on three different charges? And what do I get in return? I get testimony on a man who *may* have been involved in one crime, and all I get then is doubtful testimony from a petty con man, trying to save his own hide?"

He looked at Barney and said, "What's wrong with this picture? Should I jump on this deal or what?"

Barney smiled. "You mean, you see a problem with the offer?"

"Well, Dave, silly as I may be, I'm going to pass on your fine offer for the time being. I expect to have both of you in jail in the near future, and, in the meantime, our tourists are going to be much safer with you out of circulation. You should have confined your activities to petty con jobs on people who weren't going to stay around long enough to file charges."

Buck shifted his attention to Raul. "Book him on all of the charges I just mentioned."

He turned back to Dave. "Have a nice day."

Buck chuckled at the sound of Dave mumbling to himself as Raul led him off for booking. Buck turned back to the highway patrolman, "Sandy, anything on the other guy, Lee Bob Courtland?"

"We found his car out on the interstate. We figure he started hitching rides there. There's nothing wrong with the car, so he must have figured it would be easy to spot. If he's hitching back to Tennessee, we'll pick him up somewhere along the way, don't worry."

Buck thanked him and went out to his car. It had been a long night, but he still had a stop to make before he could go home to get some rest, and that was the hospital.

Doc was taping Little Bear's ribs as Buck came in. Buck asked about him.

"He's okay. He got some cracked ribs, so he'll be on light duty for a couple of weeks."

"Well, he got it in the line of duty, so he'll get paid while he recovers."

"Would you two quit talking about me like I'm not here."

Buck smiled. "Are you in much pain?"

"Not much. I get a twinge if I bend over or pick something up, but as long as I get around slowly, it's all right. If you don't mind, I thought I'd like to go up to your cabin and spend the two weeks Doc is talking about, doing a little quiet fishing."

"Okay by me. You want some company?"

"Don't mean to hurt your feelings, old friend, but I think I'd like to have some time alone."

"No problem I really have too much to do right now anyway, but I would have gone if you'd needed me. In fact, I was going to ask you to go to the place where they found Courtland's car to see if you could tell anything about the tracks, but I guess you're too sore to do it."

"I am pretty sore, but I'll take a look if you need me to. I have to tell you though that all I'll probably find are tracks to where he got into some car, then nothing after that."

"No point in making you hurt for no more than that."

"Be glad to do it if you think it's worth your while."

"No, never mind, you go relax and pull yourself back together."

◊

Little Bear went to the store, got two big boxes of provisions, and had these loaded into his old truck. He drove to the ranch, where a couple of hands saddled a horse for him and loaded his provisions on a pack horse.

"How you gonna get this stuff off when you get up there? A ranch hand said. "Need one of us to go with you and get you settled in?"

"No, thanks a lot, but I have gravity to help me up there. It's hard to get a saddle or provisions up on a horse, but it only takes a jerk on a knot to get it down. I'll simply drop it on the back porch and use it from there." He stepped up onto the horse with a groan, took a couple of deep breaths to clear his head from the effort, then pointed the horses up the trail, waving as he left and thanking them for their help.

He let the horses amble along in a leisurely walk. The sun shone on him, bringing warmth to his aching muscles.

Just shy of the turn up to the cabin, he forked off the trail, and soon picked up some fresh tracks. He pulled up short of the rock shelf under the cliff.

In a loud voice he said, "Lee Bob, I know you're up there! If you don't answer, I'm gonna drop you off some provisions and ride on. But if you'd like you can come to the cabin with me and we'll spend a couple of pleasant weeks fishing while you wait for the heat to blow over."

"That you, Little Bear?"

He chuckled, "What's left of me after your tree got through with me."

"You sore about that?"

"If you mean am I mad, the answer is no. If you mean physically sore, the answer is yes."

"I'm downright sorry about that," Lee Bob said as he climbed down.

"It was all in the game."

"How'd you know I was here?"

"No mountain man would try to make a run for it in the flatlands with somebody after him. These were the nearest mountains. How'd you get here?"

"I left the car where they would search for me on the interstate going home, then I walked back to the highway coming here and hitched a ride."

"I thought so. I didn't want to lie to the sheriff, so I told him all he'd find were tracks leading to where you got in a car. I forgot to mention I thought it'd be on a different highway. I'd have had to tell him that if he'd asked me." He glanced up at the cliff. "How'd you find this place?"

"I knew there had to be a good hiding place somewhere along the trial you took the other day since I didn't find you. It wasn't too tough to find once I got right down to it."

"Think you can climb up on top of those supplies for a few miles? We can head over to the cabin."

"I think we'd make better time with me on foot. I'm used to it." He gave Little Bear a questioning look. "You sure you aren't going to turn me in?"

"Just because you were *thinking* about doing something bad? You didn't do it when the chips were down. Besides, a fellow told me once there weren't enough mountain men left that we can afford to lose one."

They started off down the trail, and Little Bear added a postscript: "Of course, there's always the fact that I need you to unsaddle this horse and unload these provisions. My ribs are sore."

Lee Bob smiled. "I guess I owe you that much, all right."

Chapter 31

Buck yawned and lay down for a minute or two before the afternoon gathering. He woke to find Doc, Barney, Wayne, and Junior already on the porch. Buck sighed as he dropped into his chair. "Wow, I hadn't planned to sleep that long, I just laid down for a minute. But that was one busy night last night."

Wayne said, "Looks like you made everything come out all right, though."

"I'd have to say there was more than a little luck involved."

Junior leaned forward and put his elbows on his knees. "If this Lee Bob fellow wasn't really a good boy at heart, we'd have bought the farm. I don't think we can count on being so lucky again."

Buck suddenly felt tired again. "Oh, yes, the next time. We need to see if we can't find a way to see there is no next time."

"I don't think there's any way, Buck, unless I come up dead."

Barney nodded, "Maybe there's the answer. Why don't we let out the story that the hit in the jail was successful? I'd be glad to run the story. I'd even let Junior write his own obituary, so it'd say exactly what he wanted it to say."

"Man doesn't get the chance to write his own obituary very often." The idea seemed to appeal to Junior.

Buck considered it, "Not a bad idea, Barney. We'll have to think on it some. Right off the top of my head, there are a couple of things which bother me about it, though."

"What's that, Buck?"

"Mostly the number of people who know it didn't happen, and we're fixing to send one of them to prison where he can put the information straight on the grapevine. There's another one running around loose, too."

Doc agreed. "There's Jim Minor running around shooting his mouth off as well."

"Yes, that too, not to mention a score of good meaning folks who under some circumstances might let it slip to the wrong party." He paused a minute or so. "Well, let's think on it some. There has to be a way."

"In the meantime," Barney said, "you have another little pressing problem,"

"The election?"

"Yes, even more so, the candidate forum tomorrow night."

"So what's the problem?" Doc shrugged. "Buck will have them eating out of his hand as usual."

"I don't know, Doc," Barney responded. "Minor isn't going to be a problem. He's got lots of money, but he hasn't lived here very long, and people around here are funny about that."

"I repeat, so what's the problem?"

"Raul. He's the problem."

"I forgot about Raul. Say, where is he tonight?"

Barney made a one handed gesture pointing East. "He's at a social over at the Catholic Church. He's got a lot of support."

Buck smiled, "It may be his time, boys. It has to come someday."

Doc scowled. "But not now, Buck. You're in your prime, and you've really done a great job; lately more than ever."

"Thanks, Doc, but it's up to the voters. They pay their money, and they get to take their choice."

◊

Mike Milner, the manager of the chamber of commerce was serving as the moderator for the debate. He got the attention of the crowd and said, "Tonight's event is sponsored by The League of Women Voters and the Chamber of Commerce. We have three people vying for mayor, two for state representative, three running for sheriff and five running for two city council positions."

"The format will be simple People have written their questions on three-by-five cards. I will then read the questions to the candidates. Our local media are sitting at the table here with me as are Barney Hoke from the newspaper, Sam Donovan from the radio station, and John Pittman, who was a stringer for several big city media. These three will be allowed to ask questions directly. Are there any questions?"

The debate was spirited but uneventful. These candidates were known to all and most had even run against each other before. The main event tonight would be the sheriff's race and everyone knew it. They had scheduled that segment last to hold the crowd. Finally it came time for that portion of the event.

The moderator started with Buck. "As the incumbent, Sheriff, you get the chance to go first. Each of you will be given the chance to make a short statement, then we will begin with the questions. Go ahead, Buck."

Buck stood and held his new hat in his hands. He smiled a shy smile and nodded. "It's a wonder I ever get elected, I'm so uncomfortable speaking to folks in groups, well," he grinned, "unless it's from the pulpit. Add to that the fact that I'm naturally kind of modest and not very much disposed to talk about myself, and it really makes things such as this tough."

Buck looked around the room to see lots of supportive smiles on faces. He resumed. "As to why you ought to vote for me for sheriff, I reckon I gotta stand on my record. Folks out this way generally don't fix something that ain't broke. I've been your sheriff over 20 years. I've pampered your kids and wiped their noses. I've found your stuff when it was missing. We've hardly had an unsolved crime while I've been sheriff. Oh, we've had some stuff simply show back up after it had turned up gone, so we just let things lie, but we all know about that."

There were a lot of knowing grins. "Over the years, I've refereed your fights, listened to your problems, and handled problems with your kids. I guess what I really hope is that I've been more than your sheriff. I hope I've been a friend."

He sat down amid thunderous applause.

"Mr. Minor, your statement please."

"My name is Jim Minor. I made my money hauling waste in Houston. I started out driving one garbage truck with a big mortgage. I built the business to where I had hundreds of trucks before I sold it. I came out here and bought a ranch. You can't serve people in a more humble capacity than hauling their garbage for them. That's what I want to do for you, handle your garbage.

"Why do I want to be sheriff? I know how to deal with people, and I know how to get the most out of your tax dollars. I've never been a cop, but we hire experienced law enforcement people. The top man doesn't have to be a cop, but he needs to be an efficient and capable administrator. There are a couple of million dollars in the bank here that testify to my ability to do that.

"Buck has done a good job. I don't deny it, in fact, I applaud him for it. But with all due respect, times are changing. You've never had a murder here before, and the drugs and other problems that have arisen are new. Also with due respect, Raul Fernandez is one fine chief deputy, but he has no experience in handling the department. This is no longer a matter of kissing babies and wiping noses, and is certainly no place for a man who is more preacher than law officer. Today you need a hard-nosed administrator to bring your sheriff's department into the twentieth century. You need me."

There was cheering and applause, which, for the most part was, well, polite. Buck sat back and waited.

"Mr. Fernandez, your statement please."

"I want to be sheriff. I didn't know how much until I started talking to people about it and saw how it felt to be running for it. Contrary to what Mr. Minor said, I am capable of running the department. I'm capable of it because Buck trained me that way. He hasn't treated me as an employee, but as a protégé. I'm capable of being sheriff because Buck taught me everything I know."

There was a buzz in the crowd as Raul went on. "The problem is Buck hasn't taught me everything *he* knows. I do want to be sheriff, and I want every one of you to remember it, but there is no reason to settle for the protégé when the good-as-new original is still available. Buck still has a lot to teach, and I want to be there to learn it, so for that reason I withdraw my name from the race."

The crowd jumped to its feet, yelling its approval. The moderator gaveled for attention, and Raul added one last line. "But when the time comes for Buck to step down, I serve my notice now that I want to be your sheriff and I *will* be ready when the time comes."

Raul didn't sit back down on the stage, but walked down into the audience. He made his way slowly to the back as everyone wanted to shake his hand or pat him on the back. People seemed to feel a big man had just gotten a lot bigger. Buck agreed with them.

It took the moderator several minutes to restore order. "We move now to the question-and-answer period. The first question is addressed to Sheriff Green. It asks why you started carrying a gun when you said it wasn't appropriate for so long?"

Buck grinned a sheepish grin. "It's not exactly a national security secret. I reckon everybody knows how I feel about a hand gun. As a preacher I didn't feel carrying one was appropriate." He looked out at Raul. "But not only did Raul learn some things from me, I've learned from him too. He made me see that citizens needed to feel their Sheriff could step in to protect them if the situation arose and he told me my congregation would understand and accept it. I've talked to them and he was right."

A subdued murmur went through the crowd, then the moderator said. "Mr. Minor, this one is for you. It asks how you can be a full time sheriff when you have a big ranch to run."

"A good question. Actually, the ranch is simply an investment. I have lots of good people who know their jobs and run it for me. I merely make overall decisions, then delegate the work to people who are experienced and qualified to do it, much as I think it should be done in the sheriff's office."

The moderator looked at another card. "It's addressed to you, Sheriff. How can you possibly wear a badge and be a pastor at the same time? Aren't the two jobs completely at odds with each other?"

Buck ….. "Some people take to law enforcement because they like authority, and they like to be able to punish people. They write tickets to punish folks, they arrest people to punish them. For them, it's all about hurting people. I don't see it the same way. For me, both jobs give me a chance to help folks, and what one doesn't offer in the way of opportunities, the other does. Come to think of it, there aren't too many jobs that can't be done by a good Christian man in a good Christian way." He looked at his opponent. "Even waste disposal."

Chapter 32

Buck knew the porch group would be eaten up with curiosity. He didn't travel much, and this time he'd been gone for four days. Raul had picked him up at the airport, and the group awaited their briefing. He grinned as he climbed out of Raul's truck.

They exchanged greetings, and he and Raul foraged in his refrigerator for drinks. Barney fidgeted… "Okay, Buck, how do you want to play it? You want to tell us what you've been up to, or do we play twenty questions until we get warm?"

"I took a little trip over to see the warden at the federal prison at Big Spring. Then I went up to the federal prison at Ottisville, New York, and talked to the warden there."

"Yeah," Doc said, "You shopping for a retirement home?"

"No, although those places are nice enough."

"Doesn't sound like it would be too comfortable for a cop to go to one of those places," Barney said.

"It would be safer there than at Huntsville. I put too many people in the state pen. I don't know why, but we don't have too many folks breaking federal crimes around here."

"All right, nineteen more questions to go." Doc sighed. "Is it animal, vegetable, or mineral?"

"Doc's right," Barney said, "Are you really going to make us pull it out of you a word at a time?"

"No, I guess not. Ottisville is where this DeGrassi character is.

The guy that's causing all of the trouble for Junior."

"Which means it's animal. Is it bigger than a bread box?"

"Sarcasm doesn't become you, Barney. I'm trying to cut a deal to get DeGrassi away from all those gangsters who support him in Ottisville. Without all of those people who are connected to the mob, I think he'd be small potatoes."

"So, how did they respond?"

"The warden over at Big Spring has a prisoner causing him a lot of trouble. Seems that guy has a lot of people on the inside over whom he can exercise control. Both wardens think they'd like to get these guys away from all of their inside support, make conditions better for everyone. Together we managed to get a Federal judge to order it."

Junior said, "Good thinking, Buck, but if they still have a telephone in the place it doesn't solve my problem."

"One thing at a time, Junior, one thing at a time."

◊

It was early evening when Buck walked in the front door of his cabin and found Lee Bob and Little Bear in front of the fireplace, drinking coffee and swapping lies. Lee Bob looked like he had been hit in the face with a wet fish.

Little Bear broke the silence. "Well, Buck, I have to admit I didn't think you would come. I felt you knew, but I didn't think you'd come."

Buck poured a cup of coffee and sat down. "Well, I ain't completely sure I'm here, Little Bear. I thought maybe you and I would have us a little talk. You see, I'm suspicious Lee Bob might be up here in the mountains somewhere, and, if he is, I calculate you might be able to get word to him. If you aren't too sore, that is."

Scarcely five foot away Lee Bob's mouth dropped open and his eyes widened. Buck still had not acknowledged the man or even looked in his direction.

Little Bear got it, "If he is here, I'm sure I could contact him."

"I have an idea which *might* get him off the hook with the gangsters. No promises, but I'm thinking it might work."

"I see. This is something he would be glad to hear."

Buck sat down facing Little Bear, his back to Lee Bob. "What he's doing now will leave him dodging the law all of his life. There's a grand jury session tomorrow, and I'm going to be testifying. The DA and I have agreed that there's no evidence to support an attempted murder charge since there's nothing to show anyone actually made a threat. There may have been intent, but if we could be tried for what we thought about doing, we'd all be in jail."

He went on. "Dave is going to be charged with several counts of contributing to the delinquency of a minor and with attempted robbery of the bank."

Lee Bob said, "I can't let you do that, Sheriff. He was only helping me."

Buck looked at the door. "I thought I heard something. Must have been the wind. Do you know whether Lee Bob actually knew what sort of diversion Dave was planning or not?"

Lee Bob said, "No, actually I didn't. He said to leave it to him. I thought he was only going to pay those kids to get into a big fight."

Little Bear said, "I think I can safely say Lee Bob did not know."

"Exactly what I thought. If Lee Bob would give evidence to the grand jury, I could offer him immunity."

"No! I ain't testifying against Dave."

"On reflection, perhaps I should state it more clearly. If Lee Bob would testify he had no prior knowledge of what Dave planned, but would refuse to testify against him, then the DA has indicated he would not name Lee Bob in the other charges."

Little Bear shifted in his chair, "I take it there is still ample testimony to bring Dave to trial?"

"Dang it! This ain't fair."

Buck ignored him. "Yes. The young people will send him to jail regardless of what Lee Bob might or might not do. However, if Lee Bob is in the trial, there is always the chance the attempted murder issue might come up. Dave knows this, and he is more than willing for Lee Bob to stay out of the trial with him."

The Indian smirked. "So what do you want me to tell Lee Bob?"

"Tell him it would be a very good idea to give himself up and face the grand jury tomorrow."

"And if he doesn't?"

"Then he's going to be ducking the law for the rest of his days, and he had better clear out of this area quickly, before I have to come looking for him."

"Makes sense to me, Sheriff. I give up."

Buck put the most genuine look of surprise on his face. "Why,

Lee Bob, what a surprise. Where did you come from?"

◊

The battleground turned out to be the front page of the newspaper. In spite of Barney's friendship, Buck figured he reported the various candidates' in a fairly objective manner.

At the Evening Jaycees, Minor alleged that Buck was slippery and that Buck had managed to make his protection of criminals look noble and self-sacrificing. He claimed Buck's good-old-boy demeanor was a front and that underneath Buck was cool and calculating and didn't care nearly as much about people as he pretended.

Buck hung his head. "It's true, everything Minor said is true. I openly admit I'm not Will Rogers, and my country-boy appearance is only an act. I never thought it'd get out, but I do wear a tuxedo around the house. I do have a degree in nuclear physics that I've been able to successfully hide all of these years, and I have to sneak off to go down and work on the space shuttle program."

"See." Minor said, "that's exactly what I'm talking about."

"He's right. I'm so ashamed. I'm not really a cowboy, and those roping trophies Jiggs and I won were put-up jobs, done with smoke and mirrors. I guess the thing that shames me the most is... " he paused as if he had completely broken down... "all right, I'll say it... I've never hauled garbage." He wiped his eyes with a big red bandanna and honked his nose. "I never thought I'd admit that in public."

Minor looked out over the crowd at all of the snickers and smiles. "I'm trying to be serious here. He's making a mockery of this whole race."

"A mockery? I'm trying to come clean here. All of the years I've worked on the United Way, the Children's Home, the Hospital Board, Crime Stoppers, the Boys Club, the rodeo, and all that other stuff? Well, Minor's right, it's all been a front. It's all been a blatant grab for votes. I know those kids will be voting age in another eight or ten years, and I'm trying to lock in their votes to perpetuate my dynasty."

Minor's voice was getting high pitched with frustration. "Everybody has skeletons in their closet but nobody seems to want to look into Buck's closet. I'm betting he has plenty to hide."

"What can I say, he's right. It has all been about money, I can admit it now. I've been squirreling away money for years, and a deep financial probe will turn up the fact that between my pension and Social Security I'm going to be living off the fat of the land. Estimates are it may be as high as three thousand a month, and I've managed to put all of it away right in front of your nose. It's amazing it only took me twenty six years to do it, isn't it?"

Everyone looked back at Minor for a response but he seemed to not be able to come up with anything further to say.

Chapter 33

Buck called Junior early one morning and said, "You want to drive over to Big Spring with me?"

"What for?"

"Your friend DeGrassi is over there now."

"I got nothing to say to him."

"I don't want you to talk to him, I've got something else in mind."

"What?"

"Let's talk on the way."

"Sure, I got nothing else to do. This ranch will run itself. It's sure enough proved that."

The prison facility in Big Spring was converted from a former Air Force base. Along with the a number of new buildings, it was neat and clean and beautifully maintained. The warden met them at the front, and Buck introduced him to Junior.

"I've heard about your problem," the warden said. "It's not right for you to have to go through all of this when you're trying to do the right thing. Well, Buck may have the answer for it. We'll see. I've got the group of inmates you wanted over in one of the classrooms. If you'll follow Jerry here, he'll take you over."

When they entered the classroom, a big grin split Junior's face. "Slim, Candy, Dodger, you old horse thief…"

The one he called Dodger grimaced and put his finger in front of his lips. "Shhh, Junior, dang it. They don't know about that one

236

here."

Junior glanced around the room to find a dozen other cowboys from the rodeo circuit. Even while he'd worked in New York, he had often taken time off to go do some rodeoing. These were good friends. "I can't believe you guys are in here. What did you do?"

"Nothing big. Various small lapses of judgment, generally associated with keeping the old home place. Except for Slim. He made dog food out of a guy he caught with his wife. He's gonna be here for a long time, which is why he's been the spokesman."

"Spokesman? I don't understand."

Slim spoke up, "We had a little talk with this DeGrassi character. We let him know he doesn't have his gang behind him anymore. Told him you are a friend of ours, and if one person shows up around your place who even looks like he may have once met DeGrassi in a restaurant, DeGrassi was going to soak up a chiv in the exercise yard."

"You'd do that?"

"Who knows? It's only important for him to believe we would. With his background, he believes it. In a few short days, he's had skin carved off his ribs four times as a warning. He's a believer."

"Do you really think he'll cancel the contract?"

"He already has. We threw in that Lee Bob fellow for good measure."

Junior looked at Buck, who waved him off. "Don't look at me. I'm not here, and I didn't hear any of this. I need to point out that the warden doesn't know anything about it either, other than to be aware the boys are putting the fear into DeGrassi. The truth is, he doesn't even really know that. If you know what I mean."

"You're some piece of work, Buck."

The warden met them again on the way out. "How'd it go?"

"I think the mission was successful."

"There's been some sort of trouble in the yard. This DeGrassi character keeps turning up in the dispensary. I think I may have to do a good unit search over there."

"It'd probably be a good idea, warden, although I think you'll find it's clean as a whistle."

"Good, I hope so."

"I think you'll also find DeGrassi will become a model prisoner. But, listen. If he starts getting visitors from back east, I'd kinda like to know about it."

"Sure thing, Sheriff. If I really knew what you've been up to, which I don't, I suspect I suggest that justice is sometimes served in unusual ways. However, even though I don't know what you're up to, I know your reputation, and I have no doubt justice *is* being served."

"Thanks, warden. If it has been served, you're the one who made it happen, even without officially knowing anything."

The warden clasped Buck by the shoulder. "I hope so. I do some of my best work when I don't know what I'm doing. You boys got time for a little lunch? We set a pretty good table here."

"I'm always up for lunch, aren't you Junior?"

"Lead me to it."

Buck and Junior returned home to find the group waiting on the porch, with Lee Bob sitting in one of the metal lawn chairs by the railing. They started in on Buck and Junior even before they sat down. Doc opened it up. "So how'd it go?"

Buck headed to the fridge. "Hold on a sec. Give us a chance to get us something cold to drink."

They got a soda and grabbed a couple of chairs. Buck was barely seated before Doc repeated, "So?"

"It went exactly as I hoped. The boys at the pen got DeGrassi to lift the contract not only on Junior, but on Lee Bob as well."

Lee Bob gave a rebel yell and followed it up with, "It was almost too much to hope for."

Junior said, "It couldn't have gone any other way. Buck had it set like bear grease in a frying pan, it went down so-o-o-o-o slick." He slapped his knee and laughed as he told the story.

They sat there a while and Little Bear said, "There are some good men down there in that place. It is a shame they got themselves there."

"Yeah, it is, although most of them aren't in for very long."

"How does a cowboy run into problems with federal law?"

"They don't account for their money, don't pay taxes right, and next thing you know, they're in trouble. Either that or they get into some fairly small scam that crosses state lines, or maybe they borrow something for a while and forget to return it."

"A real shame…" one said, and the chorus followed suit.

"Sure is."

"Dirty shame."

"Sure hate to see it."

Buck changed the subject. "So, Lee Bob, how about this? You getting to sit right out here on the porch like a real human being."

"Yeah, thanks to you. It still doesn't feel quite right for me to walk, and old Dave go to jail."

"If it helps ease your mind, we've been trying to get Dave on something for several years. He may not be going up as much for this as he is for all of the things he's been getting away with."

He shook his head slowly, "Maybe so, but it still doesn't feel right."

"Do you know what you're going to do yet? Are you going back home?"

He straightened up and his face brightened. "You know, folks have been so good to me out here, I thought I might see if I could get me a job here."

Junior said, "Know anything about cows?"

"Some."

"Some is enough. I need a ranch hand."

Buck said, "Where's Jack?"

Junior laughed. "Didn't you hear? He left town right after the UFO thing. He said my place was too weird for him, what with gangsters and UFO's and tracks to nowhere. He didn't stay out there anyway. He was only a day hand. I need a full-time ranch hand."

Lee Bob seemed confused. "Why me? After all, I did come here with my sights set on you."

"Yeah, you got off course for a little while, but when it got right down to it, we found out what you were made of. I'd rather have a man who's tested and true than one who looks good on paper but may not prove out. Besides, if somebody shows up looking for me, they'll be looking for you, too. We might as well watch each other's back."

Lee Bob put on a broad grin. "It passes muster for me. I'll make you a good hand."

Junior stood and offered his hand. "I know you will, Lee Bob, I know you will."

After he shook Lee Bob's hand he turned, "So how about you, Buck? You going to take some time off now that you got it all wrapped up?"

"All wrapped up? I don't know about that. There's always something to do around this place. Wayne, you remember I told you life is just working down your list?"

"Yes, and you said there was only one way to finish the list."

"Right, and given that choice, I'm glad to have things on my list to do."

Doc said, "You've got a little campaigning to do yet, as well."

"True, but I'm not doing any more debates. I'm not fighting verbal battles in the paper either. I'm going back to what's always worked for me."

"Kissing babies?"

"You got it."

"Wouldn't hurt to play it safe, but, from all I hear, Minor shot up all his ammunition in the last round. It finished him off. He doesn't even have the heart for it now."

"Maybe so, I guess we'll see."

They sat in silence for a while before Doc said, "You seem to have gotten everything wrapped up for everybody else, Buck, how about for you?"

"What do you mean?"

"Hey, this is me. Doc. I know the battle you've been having

trying to balance serving both the badge and the Bible. I heard your comments in the election debates and it made it sound like you had everything in balance, but I know better. I know it's something you wrestle with all the time."

Everyone on the porch was silent, watching Buck closely. They all knew the truth of what Doc came right out and put into words.

Buck weighed his words for several minutes as they waited, knowing what he was doing. "I make choices on a daily basis like when I made the decision to start wearing a sidearm. So far, I'm not finding that my choices represent a major conflict."

Barney said, "I can see that. I don't see a lawman having good, Christian principles as being a liability."

Wayne added, "And there's sure no problem with a preacher believing in law and order."

Doc wouldn't let it go. "But everything is not as black and white as it used to be. Federal laws are causing us to question some of the laws we're asked to obey. Things are changing. I suppose the big question is, if you do come to a situation where there is a direct conflict between the two roles, what happens then?"

Buck looked up with a small smile. "Absolutely no question, I throw the badge and the gun on the desk and walk away… and never look back.

Please enjoy a preview of Terry's book, *Saint's Roost.* If you enjoyed *The Badge and the Bible,* please consider leaving a review for other readers on Terry's Amazon Author Page.

Chapter One

1879 Santa Fe Trail

A   wagon leaving the safety of a wagon train to strike out by itself is a lonesome sight.

Its occupants, Patrick and Janie Benedict were headed west in an old Conestoga that complained at every bump and jolt in the road. The wheels squealed a high-pitched, irritating sound. Still, it was marginally dependable. More dependable were the four Missouri mules that drew it, depending on their mood and disposition at the moment.

The young couple looked the part, him tall and handsome with the sincere brown eyes appropriate for a young minister. The prairie heat made shirtsleeves mandatory and he peered out from under a flat-brimmed black hat indicative of those who pursued the avocation of a circuit-riding preacher.

His bride of only a year sat next to him, simply clad in a checked dress and plain white bonnet. Her hair peeked out from the bonnet and lit up scarlet red when the sun touched it. Both their faces were brighter from barely contained excitement and enthusiasm than from the rays of the hot summer sun.

They made the trek west because Patrick had been called to the ministry. More specifically, he had felt himself called to do missionary work in what he referred to as the wild, wild West. Not that he had to go so far to find sinners; there was certainly more sin right there in certain sections of St. Louis than would be found in the entire west.

Yet many of his seminary classmates knew that in the secret compartments of his mind, Patrick saw himself in a saintly pose, surrounded by a throng of half-naked savages kneeling about him as he converted them in droves by the power of his magnificent oratory. Such ambitious visions were certainly encouraged at the seminary.

Still, some of his teachers thought him very naive. Others thought him to be headstrong while the more optimistic conceded he had a *unique evangelistic drive*. The term the wagon master came up with when a couple of young people still in their twenties left the train alone was...well...to be truthful...stupid.

◊

Quite a distance back up the wagon trail, pint-size Ruben Dunn had his own ideas. He had these ideas on virtually any subject you could name, and he didn't mind sharing them with anyone inclined to listen.

Ruben's alter ego and long-time saddle mate was a tall drink of water by the name of Frank Walker. Had Frank ever been caught asleep at the wrong place, someone might have mistakenly used him to try and repair a length of split rail fence. Frank had dark hair that defied any comb in existence, chocolate brown eyes, and was unfailingly good humored and easy going.

More important, and absolutely essential to have a friendship with Ruben, he knew his own mind and did not feel it necessary to debate various points with his confident, but diminutive companion. Once Frank made up his mind, he simply went ahead and did what he wanted without much, if any, discussion.

Ruben on the other hand could debate the finer points of doing something different the entire time he calmly followed Frank's lead. The fact that he espoused one course of action while he did another never seemed to be a problem, it was merely how life worked. It certainly had nothing to do with diluting the opinions Ruben might hold.

At the present time the pair drifted with no particular destination in mind. Ruben did have some thoughts on where they should go and what they should do, however. He tipped his hat back on his head to reveal a shock of blonde hair with the look and consistency of prairie straw. He squeezed off his ever-present grin to compress his face into a more thoughtful expression, closed both hands on top of his saddle horn and ventured his opinion.

"What I think," Ruben said, "is we could get us a ranch started down Texas way. There's loose stock, mavericks they call them, all over the place, and they're ours for the taking if we want to put up the hard work. There's land available that can be had mighty cheap. The land of opportunity, that's what they call it, and that's what it is. We could call our ranch the Dunn-it ranch. I can almost see the sign over the gate," he looked off into the distance as if he could see the very sight he was describing.

"You being the Dunn and me being the *it*, I suppose." No trace of emotion showed on Frank's face to indicate whether he might be kidding or not.

Ruben grimaced, "Aw, Frank, it ain't like that, it ain't like that at all, it's just a catchy name."

"If we branded cows with Dunn-it, they'd be barbequed while they was still on the hoof."

"Dang it, Frank, you got no imagination." Ruben let go of the saddle horn and poked the air vigorously in his partner's general direction to emphasize his point.

"That ain't so, and you know it. I ain't even hung up on a name, I just like to twist your tail a little ever' now and then. Keeps you humble." Frank may have had a hint of a smile on his face. With him it was hard to tell.

"I don't think it's possible to keep me humble, me being so nacherly great and all."

"On further thought, I kinda like the name. It'd make people feel sorry for me with what I have to put up with. You know, me being an 'it' would be plain enough for anybody." Ruben only looked at him as if unable to comprehend as he shook his head slowly side to side.

◊

"Janie," Patrick rested his hands on his knees, keeping gentle pressure on the reins. "I can hardly wait. I know I've been called to do great things. I tell you I'll convert so many of these heathens..."

Janie smiled, she had heard this day and night for a year, but she didn't mind. She was proud of the man she thought of as her young knight, and believed in his quest as strongly as he did. She had no doubt but what he would do exactly as he said he would do.

All the way down through Kansas he practiced his oratory, and he wrote sermons: moving, and powerful if flowery sermons. His only congregation for these epistles, besides Janie, were the four Missouri mules. There was no record as to whether he converted them or not, as they were notoriously uncommunicative. The evidence certainly proved him to be a patient and pious man, however, as anyone who can drive a brace of such animals without the fortification of stout teamster cusswords, was a man of strong character, indeed.

Clearing the Kansas line took them into Indian Territory.

It was intentional. The wagon train had been primarily commercial and they felt out of place. The word going around was the railroad to Santa Fe was nearing completion and would soon replace the wagon trail entirely. Too much civilization, surely the unchurched Indians he searched for would be down in the territory.

Had they come straight down from St. Louis, it would have put them over in the country occupied by the Five Civilized Tribes. The tribes in that part of the territory were known for establishing farms and towns, and had centuries of beliefs and customs of their own which did not conflict strongly with Christian beliefs. It would have been fertile ground for Patrick's work.

But they didn't come directly south. They had consistently veered off to the right, and by the time they got through Kansas, they were well into the part of the territory known as no-man's land. It was a land inhabited by outlaws, and the Comanche and Kiowa, who roamed across the plains of Texas all the way up into western Kansas. Here, indeed, were exactly the inveterate sinners and naked savages Patrick had envisioned, and in quantities sufficient to fulfill any dream he may have had.

It was mid-morning when they met their first opportunity to start his ministry. They topped a small rise in the sea of blowing grass they had been in for days. Suddenly, they saw ahead of them two magnificent mounted warriors on painted ponies.

They were tall, and naked to the sun except for a breechcloth and moccasins on their feet. Their faces were painted, and on their heads were feathered bonnets, which trailed well down their backs. They held shields with bright painted symbols on them in their left hands.

Patrick was elated. His first prospects. And exactly what he had envisioned in his dreams. He pulled the team up about 50 yards away, dismounted and tied them off to a ground hitch weight. The warriors watched curiously. He slipped into his black frock coat, picked up and clutched his Bible to his chest and started toward them with his hand held up in a sign of peace.

His smile was still fixed on his face when the arrow drove deep into his chest.

The great sermon he had practiced so long remained caught in his throat. His mind screamed, *No! I can't be denied my destiny. Janie,.. what will—*

Then he fell over on his face, and the last of his air gently left him as he went on to his reward.

ABOUT THE AUTHOR

Terry was a literary agent with the Hartline agency for over twelve years, seven years as an agent, with a reputation for presenting to conferences all over the country. Terry comes from a writing background, has over 40 books of his own in print, most recently writing the western ***Hounded,*** and co-writing ***Writing in Obedience*** with editorial assistant Linda Yezak. He wrote the Christian western e book ***Mysterious Ways*** series, a Young Adult entitled ***Beyond the Smoke,*** which won the Will Rogers Medallion and a book on the skills needed to get published entitled ***"A Writer's Survival Guide to Publication"*** that was developed out of the month long course he held for ACFW. A bookstore of his available works as well as a periodic blog can be found at www.terryburns.net.